Ride
or Die

"Newman takes what, on the barest surface, seems nothing more than a suburban teen drama, and viciously rips it wide open, exposing the entrails in its pitch-black theme of vengeance and in its wildly twisted revelations. It will leave you rattled to the core."

– Kenzie Jennings (*Reception*; *Red Station*)

"*Ride or Die* depicts humanity at its best and worst with the worst being something we all hope and pray to never meet ourselves. I guarantee you'll be breathless by the last page. Horror fans are in for a real treat with this book and will forever cast a sideways glance at any street sign for Callaghan Drive after reading it."

– Somer Canon (*Killer Chronicles*; *The Hag of Tripp Creek*)

"With *Ride or Die*, Newman delivers a gut-punch of a story. Powerful, intense, exciting . . . this one has all the right ingredients and Newman is one hell of a chef!"

– Mark Allan Gunnells (*324 Abercorn*; *Before He Wakes*)

"Amelia's dad is having an affair, but she doesn't realize that revenge is a dish best served cold. When she and girlfriends decide to play a nasty prank on her dad's mistress, they bite off more than they can chew. Newman explores themes of loyalty and family amid a madcap, bloodthirsty novella that never eases off the gas."

– Kristin Dearborn (*Stolen Away*; *Whispers*)

"*Ride or Die* is a thrill ride that both excites and terrifies with each turn of the page. I read it in one sitting and absolutely loved it."

– Sarah French (star of *Blind* and *The Special*)

Ride
or Die

by
James Newman

This one's for Miranda.

If you barged in on the trio any other night and asked what they were gabbing about, *girl stuff* would have been their likeliest answer. A cryptic reply that meant nothing and everything at once. Perhaps the one whose name was painted in purple on the wall above the bed would have lobbed her plush Baby Yoda at you (they had all outgrown such toys, but she had recently admitted to the others that she could only sleep when she cuddled with it, ever since she'd learned about the thing with her father). They would squeal at you to GET OUT, and their high-pitched giggles would have echoed down the hallway as you fled in mock terror.

But that was *before*.

Amelia Fletcher and her friends found that laughter was in short supply after what happened inside the house on Callaghan Drive.

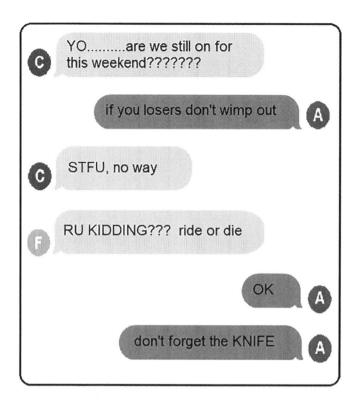

—group text message found on iPhone recovered at 47 Callaghan Drive on the morning of August 8, 2020

"I heard Mike Mitchell's penis looks like an acorn," Amelia said as she thumbed through her eighth-grade yearbook.

Cassie covered her mouth with one hand, nearly spewing Diet Coke all over her sketchpad. A plastic case full of colored pencils rattled beside her on the bed. Folline stopped painting her toenails long enough to throw back her head and laugh. Her long red hair slapped Amelia in the face.

"How would you know what Mike Mitchell's penis looks like?" Cassie asked.

"I wouldn't *know*. Just telling what I heard. Lacey Plymill was at the Y last Saturday, she told Veronica Neal she could see right up his bathing suit when he got out of the pool. Said his goober looked like a little acorn."

"*Goober*." Cassie snickered.

Folline said, "He's kinda cute. I'd probably check it out." Her name was pronounced *fallen*, but depending on her mood, she would probably let it go if you got it wrong because *everybody* got it wrong. She often insisted that her parents hated her guts—why else would they have named her Folline Raine?

For the next few seconds, the only sound was a soft *bloop* from the aquarium atop Amelia's dresser. Bradley and Gaga gawked at the girls from their side of the glass, as if Folline's confession shocked even the two bubble-eye goldfish.

"Mike Mitchell?" Cassie gasped. "You're kidding, right?"

"Nope," Folline said.

"Folline's in love with Mike Mitchell! She wants to have his babies!"

"I never said that."

Cassie wrapped her arms around herself, wagged her tongue in the air as if making out with an invisible boy. "Ohh, Mikey...can I see it? I *love* acorns. I wanna store them in my mouth for the winter, like a squirrel!"

"You are such a *beeyatch*," Folline said, as she added the finishing touches to her glittery green toenails.

Cassie laughed, brushed eraser boogers off her drawing with a flick of a wrist. Her rainbow bracelet jingled. Her current work in progress depicted Darth Vader getting his ass kicked by Wonder Woman while the Incredible Hulk sat munching on a bucket of KFC in the background. Cassie's dream was to move to the Big Apple the day she turned eighteen—two years, nine months, eleven days, and counting!—where she would land a gig with Marvel or DC the moment they peeped her skills. Cassandra McKinley was gonna be bigger than Todd McFarlane, just you wait and see.

Amelia tossed the yearbook onto her nightstand, sighed as she picked up her iPhone and checked the time. She cued up some music on Spotify, cranking the volume as loud as it would go.

"Oh, yeah!" Cassie said. "This is my jam!"

"Same," Folline said.

They sang along. Everyone except Amelia, who closed her eyes and leaned back against the headboard. Once upon a time, her voice would have been the loudest. She used to swear she was gonna win *American Idol* one day. But lately she claimed she had lost all desire to ever sing again. Hard to put on a happy face, she said, when your world was crumbling to pieces beneath your feet.

Folline and Cassie glanced at one another, wishing they could ease their friend's suffering. But this kind of pain couldn't be killed with a splash of iodine and a Band-Aid, like their mommies used to do when they were little and learning to ride their bikes in the cul-de-sac at the end of the block.

When the song was over, Cassie said, "She's playing in Greenville next month. We should go."

"We totally should," Folline said. "What do you think, Meel?"

Amelia sniffled, shrugged. The concert was scheduled for a Tuesday night and school was starting soon, which meant they were sure to miss it. Folline's big brother might have agreed to play chauffer, but he was leaving for the Army in two weeks. Cassie's folks were pretty cool, but they weren't exactly made of money. As for Amelia's parents, they had their own stuff going on. To say the least.

A breeze wafted through the open window. With it came the smell of a neighbor grilling hot dogs. The sky was the color of spring lilacs as the sun slowly dipped below the horizon.

Folline stole a sip from Cassie's can of Diet Coke, even though she had sworn less than an hour ago to never drink another soda after discovering a pimple on her chin. Cassie gnawed at her bottom lip as she fussed over some final detail on her drawing. Amelia stared out the window, watching Dr. Cannon and his wife jog by on the other side of the street with their shaggy sheepdog in tow.

"Mrs. Cannon isn't fooling anybody. Her boobs were half that size six months ago."

"Scandalous," Folline said.

"I'll bet their pool boy likes them," Amelia said, her voice cracking. "I've seen the way they look at each other. And right under her husband's nose..."

The other two dropped what they were doing to sandwich Amelia between them. They wrapped their arms around her. No one spoke for the next minute or so. True friends didn't have to say anything. They just had to *be there* for you.

"How could he *do* this to her?" Amelia sobbed.

Outside, fireflies blinked in the dusk like guests arriving early to a party yet to begin. Bass thumped on a car stereo somewhere in the distance.

"FML." Amelia used her pajama sleeve to wipe away a tear that had trickled down her cheek. "Let's do it. I'm ready."

The other two released her from their embrace.

Together they stood and bent to retrieve what lay hidden beneath Amelia's bed.

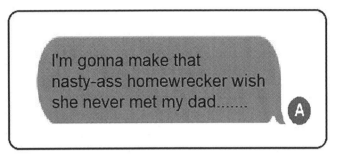

—text message found on iPhone recovered at 47 Callaghan Drive on the morning of August 8, 2020

Both of her parents were indisposed for the next couple of days. Dad had left that morning for an insurance seminar in Chicago. In his absence, Mom was pulling a double at the ER to cover for a fellow nurse who needed some time off.

Anyone who knew her would tell you Amelia didn't have a rebellious bone in her body. She remembered "getting in trouble" only once in her life (she had left her bicycle lying in the driveway and her father backed over it as he was leaving for work one morning, nearly giving Dad a heart attack and mangling her brand-new Hello Kitty BMX beyond repair). But everything had aligned so perfectly it was as though tonight's events were meant to happen. That was why she planned to do something so uncharacteristic of the Amelia Fletcher everybody thought they knew—perpetual straight-A student, chorus nerd, and don't forget would-be *American Idol* contender—and she hadn't wasted a second thinking about the consequences.

Because *this*…this demanded retaliation.

She led her friends across her backyard, past the swing set none of them had touched for years, past the peonies and begonias her mother had planted along the edge of the driveway. They were all still dressed in their slumber party attire, as they expected to be home well before midnight, their business wrapped up in record time. Amelia wore green flannel jammies. Cassie had on a Batman tank-top and gray sweatpants. Folline wore pajama shorts polka-dotted with glow-in-the-dark skulls and a Motley Crue t-shirt (she would have been hard-pressed to name one song by the band, but bought it at a thrift shop 'cause she thought its *Shout At the Devil* pentagram logo looked "cool and evil"). A motion-sensor floodlight clicked on as the teens approached a small garage at the rear of the property. Their shadows stretched out in their wake like ugly stains on something that was once spotless and immaculately maintained.

Folline and Cassie waited patiently for Amelia's next move. They each carried plastic grocery bags that strained like the bellies of pregnant spiders beneath the weight of what lay inside.

For a long moment Amelia stared at the spot where Mom usually parked her Prius, a wave of sadness washing over her. She thought about how she used to scribble with her sidewalk chalk for hours on end until a summer storm came along to wash her drawings away. She always cried when that happened until her daddy scooped her up in his arms, told her she could make new pictures, and promised next time he would make some with her. Back then life seemed so perfect. Back then it was impossible to believe your role models could ever disappoint you. *Back then I was a stupid kid who didn't have a clue about anything...*

Amelia set down her own Walmart bag. Its contents complained with a metallic *clank* upon the pavement. She dialed the numbers 9 7 7 8, the date of Keith Moon's death, on the combination padlock securing the bay door. Rolled up the door with a grunt. Picked up her bag again and stepped inside.

The garage smelled like gasoline and WD-40. In one corner stood a toolbox on wheels; in the other, a large air-compressor. An empty Coors Light bottle and a portable CD player sat atop the toolbox. Taped to the back wall was a poster of Pete Townshend windmilling away at his guitar. The Who was her father's favorite band. He had met them once when he was in college, after winning backstage passes in a radio contest, and he often said it was the greatest night of his life, second only to the night his daughter was born.

Dad's prized possession was a 1970 Plymouth Roadrunner. It sat before them, grille facing the street, in all its restored glory: Plum Crazy purple with a black stripe on the hood, chromed out from bumper to bumper, beefed-up rear end, Weld racing wheels, and a rebuilt 383 CID V8 engine. Amelia didn't understand a word of that but knew it all by heart since Dad never shut up about it. He had bought the car last winter from a guy he knew at work, and he had spent countless hours fine-tuning it to perfection. On hot nights when she slept with her window open, she often heard "Baba O'Riley" blasting out here in the garage, accompanied by the sporadic blat of an air-ratchet echoing across the driveway like the mating call of some strange nocturnal bird. It was on one of those nights, in fact, when she had discovered his dirty secret.

Amelia made a face like she had bitten into something rotten as she approached the back of the car. She had never considered its "1COOLDAD" vanity plate to be very cool to begin with, but now the sight of it made her want to vomit.

She unlocked the trunk, opened the lid. She had always known where he kept the keys. As far back as she could remember, they hung on a little hook on the wall beside the fridge, on a fob shaped like a shark. It wasn't like he even tried to hide them in plain sight. After all, he never would have suspected his fifteen-year-old daughter— straight-A student, chorus nerd, *blah, blah, blah*—would do what she was about to do.

Serves you right, Dad. I never believed you could do what you *did, either.*

She shoved aside a jack and a tire iron, dumped what she was carrying into the trunk.

"I can't believe we're gonna do this," Folline said. "Are we really gonna do this?"

"You can change your mind," Amelia said without missing a beat. "You can both stay here and I won't hold it against you."

"Screw you, hooker. We're all in this together."

"Ride or die," said Cassie.

"Good. Drop that stuff in here and let's hit the road."

"Word," said Folline. "I call shotgun!"

Once that was taken care of, Cassie climbed into the backseat, Amelia slid behind the steering wheel, and Folline claimed the bucket seat up front beside Amelia.

The Roadrunner's interior smelled like her father. Amelia swallowed a lump in her throat, remembered how she had saved up her own money to buy him a bottle of Polo Blue Sport for his birthday. *Does he wear it when he's with* her?

She fought back new tears. Took a minute to study the instrument panel in front of her before turning the key in the ignition. The Roadrunner's engine rumbled like a wild animal awakening from a long hibernation. She revved the gas.

"If we get pulled over let me do the talking," Amelia said. She was the only one among them who possessed her learner's permit, but she wasn't supposed to drive after dark, or with more than one teenage passenger in the car, and never without a parent. Not to mention she was five seconds away from committing grand theft auto. "Maybe it'll help that my cousin's with the highway patrol, maybe it won't. I don't really give a crap, if you wanna know the truth."

She revved the gas again. Adjusted the rearview mirror. Turned on the headlights.

"You're sure nobody's home, right?" Cassie said.

"I'm sure." The leather steering wheel cover squeaked in Amelia's two-handed death-grip. "She's with him, remember?"

She jammed the gearshift into drive. The Roadrunner lurched forward. The other girls wasted no time throwing on their seatbelts.

"Good thing…'cause if I ever get my hands on her, you might end up with your first client, Folline Raine."

Folline laughed uneasily. People always assumed she wanted to be a model or a Dallas Cowboys cheerleader when she grew up. Only her two best friends knew Folline's dream job was to be a medical examiner, solving violent crimes like they did on those forensic shows she loved to watch.

They turned left, out of the Fletchers' driveway.

The time was a quarter past eight. According to the Waze app on Amelia's phone, their ETA was 8:47.

She had found out about her father's affair two weeks earlier, on one of the hottest, muggiest nights of the year. It was the kind of night when the blankets stick to your sweat-soaked skin and it's not enough to throw them off your body, you have to kick them off the bed entirely so there's no chance they might touch you at all. Amelia tossed and turned, unable to sleep. But it wasn't just the midsummer heat that made her finally concede to her insomnia, grabbing her iPhone to scroll through social media as she sat beside her open bedroom window. She had been stressing out over her own problems with the opposite sex...

Tyler Thompson had transferred to her school around Christmas last year, and Amelia developed a crush on the guy from the moment she first saw him. According to Susan Wisdah, who sat beside her in social studies, the feeling was *mos def* mutual. Susan said Tyler told Bobby Gonce (Susan's guy) that Amelia was the most beautiful girl he had ever seen. A few days later, Tyler approached Cassie in art class and asked her out. Cassie told him she didn't swing that way, but gave up her best friend's digits after forcing Tyler to admit how lame it was that he only talked to her in the first place because he knew she was tight with Amelia.

They had spent countless hours on the phone ever since, strolled hand in hand around the local mall on rainy Saturday afternoons, and attended basketball games together when their Midnight Mustangs played at home. He had given her a teddy bear for Valentine's Day; a honeybee was perched on its shoulder and it held a heart in one paw that read "I CAN'T BEAR TO BEE WITHOUT YOU." During the 4th of July celebration at the city park they had swapped spit under the stars, instead of *ooh*ing and *ahh*ing at the fireworks along with everyone else (she even let him touch her boobs that night—strictly over the blouse, for the record).

But these days she was sure they were finished. Because Tyler Thompson was a grade-A butthead.

From the start of their relationship, Amelia heard rumors about how he wasn't the type of guy you should expect to be faithful. Rhonda Bailey claimed she knew Tyler's ex back home, and he had cheated on her the whole time they were together. Sophie Bullman said she spotted Tyler making out with DeeDee Youngblood under the bleachers during a pep rally, and she was "a gazillion percent sure" it was after Amelia started going out with him. Before long, Amelia started to notice his roaming eyes when another girl walked by. She finally called him on it, and he told her he didn't know if he could be with somebody who acted so freaking jelly all the time, like they were married or something.

She sat on her windowsill, chin resting on one knee, feeling super dumb for falling for a jerk like Tyler, thumbing halfheartedly at her iPhone. Every few minutes a warm breeze blew into her room, bringing with it the scents of recently-mown grass and tar (thanks to the Tierneys next door, who had repaved their driveway that morning). The two goldfish in the aquarium atop her dresser watched her from their side of the glass, as if sympathetic to her predicament. She had spoken with Tyler a couple of hours earlier but hung up on him when he accused her of acting "retarded." Meanwhile, her father was still tooling around out there in the garage at well past ten p.m. On the night in question, he worked without any music, undoubtedly because of the late hour. A gruff curse occasionally echoed across their property when he struggled with a stubborn lug nut or banged his knuckles on something under the hood. From this angle, in her second-story bedroom, she couldn't quite see inside the garage, only the light spilling from its open bay door onto the driveway. It always made her think of firelight emanating from the lair of some benevolent dragon. She liked knowing her father was out there. She felt safe, like when she was a little kid drifting off to the sound of her parents' muffled conversation through the wall as they watched their late-night talk shows. She often pondered how there couldn't be more men like her daddy. Men who were honest. *Real*. Later, she would wonder how she could have been so naïve…

She had just finished posting a selfie to Snapchat (#boyssuck, #tiredofhisBS, followed by a million sad-faced emojis) when Dad stepped out of the garage.

She slid off the windowsill, ducked out of sight. She wasn't sure why. Maybe because he could always tell when something was wrong with her. He would ask what she was "sulking" about. And she sure didn't feel like talking to her father about what was going on with Tyler Two-Face.

He stood in the middle of the driveway, looking down at his cell phone. He wore green jogging shorts, flip-flops, and an old t-shirt (BILL MURRAY INSURANCE, read the logo on his chest—he often joked that his boss wasn't the famous actor, but after working with him once his clients never had to ask "who you gonna call?"). He was a tall, handsome man with a receding hairline and a thin black beard. There was a smear of brown grease on his cheek.

He glanced toward the house, wiped his sweaty brow with a muscular forearm. A sly grin spread across his face as he brought the phone to his ear. His expression made Amelia think of a little boy who was up to no good.

"Hey," he said into the phone. "Did I wake you?"

Although he spoke in a low, conspiratorial tone, the night was still and quiet. Amelia could hear every word.

"Nothing important," he said. "I just wanted to hear your voice."

Amelia frowned. Mom had knocked on her door over an hour ago, said goodnight while she was on the phone with Tyler. So who in the world was Dad talking to?

"I can't stop thinking about you either."

Amelia watched him pace from one side of the driveway to the other, his flip-flops slapping against the soles of his feet like slow applause from an invisible spectator.

"God. I wish I was there. I want to be inside you again."

Her breath caught in her throat.

"I wish. Doubt I'll be able to sneak away this weekend, though. Family obligations. How about Monday? We could meet on my lunch break. Great. I'll see you then."

He hung up. Smiled down at the phone before slipping it into his pocket. Headed back into the garage with a strut in his step.

"*WTF?*" Amelia whispered to her reflection in the mirror on the opposite side of her bedroom.

The girl in the mirror wore a nightshirt with that same initialism printed on it in big block letters. She clutched to her bosom the teddy bear Tyler had given her for Valentine's Day. Amelia couldn't remember retrieving it from the wastebasket beneath the window, where she had slam-dunked it earlier…but now she gripped it like a drowning woman clinging to anything that might prevent the hot, heavy darkness from consuming her forever.

She hadn't thought much about Tyler after that night. His calls and texts went ignored. Tyler Thompson could mess around with whomever he wanted, or he could take a long walk off a short pier. She really didn't care either way. All Amelia could think about was what she'd heard out there in the driveway, the things Dad had said to someone who *wasn't Mom.*

It sounded ridiculous when she put it into words: *My father is having an AFFAIR. My dad is SCREWING another woman.*

Cheating happened to *other* families. Like the shenanigans she suspected had been going on all summer between Dr. Cannon's wife and their pool boy. Or that girl in her home economics class last year, Paula something, who used to be a real teacher suck-up but then she stopped washing her hair and started smelling like dirty socks all the time after she found out her parents were swingers.

What was *wrong* with him? How could he be so selfish?
She had to know more. Didn't want to. *Had* to. Dread roiled in her gut like food poisoning at the thought of it.

But she needed to destroy any shred of doubt before deciding what to do next...

It had been too easy, really. One night she waited until she heard him snoring before sneaking into her parents' bedroom to "borrow" his phone for a while. She locked herself in their downstairs bathroom, and by the glow of an air-freshener nightlight she steeled herself for the task at hand. She correctly guessed his passcode on her first attempt: her birthday.

It took her less than a minute to regret playing amateur detective...

The other woman's name was Zoe. He had met her online two months ago, in a Facebook group for classic rock fans called IF IT'S TOO LOUD YOU'RE TOO OLD. They started off as friends but flirting via FB Messenger quickly escalated into so much more when they discovered they lived less than thirty miles apart.

They had sent nearly four hundred text messages back and forth over the last eight weeks. Some of them contained photos. Dad's lover appeared to be in her early thirties, about ten years younger than him. She was a long-legged woman with pale skin, high cheekbones, and shoulder-length blonde hair that framed her face in a pageboy cut. In many of the pictures, she wore a red negligee. In most of them she wore nothing. She had small breasts with puffy pink nipples and she shaved herself down there. There were videos too. In one she performed an awkward striptease for the camera while a pop song from the '80s played in the background. In another she licked her middle finger, slid it in and out of herself without making a sound.

Dad had reciprocated with at least one photo of his own. It was a close-up of his erect penis, gripped in his palm. It was long, skinny, and bright red, as if he had just stepped out of a hot shower.

Amelia nearly dropped his phone into the toilet at the sight of it. But not before noticing he was still wearing his wedding band when he snapped his disgusting dick pic.

Next, she scrolled down to their most recent conversation, and there she had learned about Dad's plans for Chicago. He had invited his little girlfriend to join him for a "romantic weekend" in the Windy City after his upcoming seminar, and she had accepted. He even offered to pay for her airfare, but she declined ("DON'T WANT WIFEY 2 CATCH ON, DO WE?" read her text, followed by a long line of winking emojis). She asked if he was a member of the Mile-High Club. "NEGATIVE," he replied. She told him he would be soon.

He had never been to her house, apparently, nor vice versa (that, at least, was some small consolation). Judging from the messages they had exchanged prior to each of their liaisons, their favorite meeting place was a sleazy motel in a neighboring county. At one point, he had asked for his lover's address so he could pick her up on his way to the airport, and she had promptly responded with—

"—47 Callaghan Drive, in Farina. So this is where that ho-bag lives, huh?" As Folline read off their destination, Amelia's phone lit her face with an eerie bluish glow.

They had been on the road for almost twenty minutes.

"In one mile, turn right onto State Road 19," said the Waze app's robotic female voice.

"Gimme." Amelia snatched her phone back from Folline. "You're gonna make me miss the next turn."

The Roadrunner's tires hummed on the asphalt. Amelia hunched over the wheel, eyes on the road. Folline stared out her passenger-side window, watching the world pass by in a blur. In the backseat Cassie loudly popped her knuckles.

"I hate it when you do that," Folline said.

"I know," Cassie said.

They swung a right onto a narrow two-lane highway. The moon hung fat and full on the horizon, like the bright white beacon of one of Cassie's favorite superheroes calling the girls to their destiny. They passed a pool supply warehouse and a cluster of office buildings. One of the businesses, Amelia was keenly aware, was Bill Murray Insurance. She recalled from snooping on his phone that Dad had once taken his mistress there after hours ("LAST NIGHT = AMAZING," he texted her the following morning, "IT WAS A FANTASY THE WIFE NEVER LET ME INDULGE…U ROCK"). She thought about the framed photo on his desk, the one taken at Disneyland when she was six years old. Did he at least have the decency to turn it so his family faced the wall before she straddled him? What about the Father's Day card tacked to the corkboard above his Keurig machine (BEST DAD IN THE GALAXY, it read, above a commissioned Cassie McKinley original: caricatures of dad and daughter co-piloting the Millennium Falcon)—did he shove the card into a drawer before shoving into his lover?

She wondered if he even cared. If *shame* was a word that existed in the vocabulary of a man who had done the things he had done. A tear ran down her cheek. She didn't wipe it away, allowed it to tickle her chin like a phantom finger before it dripped onto her thigh.

Cassie shifted position in the back seat. The leather upholstery made a farting sound beneath her. Folline snickered, pulled her phone out of her bra, and started scrolling through social media. She mumbled something about how Tabitha Lounsberry was such a drama queen.

They travelled on through the night, leaving a vast cornfield, a tire shop, and a dilapidated fruit stand (CANALOPES $1 read the sign out front) in the Roadrunner's rearview mirror.

Folline said, "I can't wait for the new season of *The Walking Dead*. Daryl Dixon is dreamy."

"Daryl Dixon always looks like he just took a bath in motor oil," Cassie said.

"What can I say. I like the bad boys."

"If real life was a movie, Folline Raine, you would fail the Bechdel test every time."

"The what-now test?" Folline frowned back at her.

"It's this thing that measures how women are represented in fiction. Named after a cartoonist who came up with it. To pass the Bechdel test, the work has to feature at least two female characters engaged in a conversation about something other than a man."

"Nerd alert," said Folline. "Wait...what are you insinuating?"

Cassie shrugged.

Folline flipped her the bird.

Amelia heard none of their chatter. Vivid images from a recent nightmare flashed through her mind while she drove: *She shuffles into her sunlit kitchen, lured by the smell of bacon. Mom stands at the stove, humming to herself while she cooks, but when Amelia yawns "good morning" she turns around and it's not Mom...it's her. She's wearing Mom's COOKIN' UP LOVE apron and nothing underneath. She grabs Amelia's wrist and her face distorts into a demonic grin as she cackles,* I'm your mommy now, little girl!

"It's not fair! How could he *do* this to her?" She struck the steering wheel with the heel of one hand.

The car swerved. She corrected just in time to avoid a head-on collision with a pickup truck. The long, angry bleat of the other vehicle's horn receded in the distance.

"Hey, Meel?" Cassie said. "We wanna help, we really do, but maybe don't turn us into roadkill before we get there?"

"Sorry," Amelia said.

They drove on, past a seedy-looking trailer park and a convenience store called the Gas N Go. Out front of the latter, three teenage guys stood beside a mud-spattered Jeep. One of the boys squeezed his crotch through his jeans as he gassed up the vehicle, while the others doubled over with laughter at whatever their buddy was saying.

"Why do guys have to suck so bad?" said Amelia.

"They just do," Folline said. "It's a scientific fact, like your brain can't live without oxygen more for more than six minutes before irreparable damage occurs."

"Oh, but *I'm* the nerd," said Cassie.

"In one mile, turn left onto Callaghan Drive," the Waze app interjected. "Then, you will reach your destination."

"Game faces," Amelia said, gripping the steering wheel tighter than ever. "We're almost there."

—text message found on iPhone recovered at 47 Callaghan Drive on the morning of August 8, 2020

It was the only house at the end of a long, paved driveway lined with tall pine trees. A one-story bungalow, yellow with brown trim. The roof was in dire need of re-shingling. Three curved brick steps led up to a high-view storm door. Out front of the property, a tall streetlight burned brightly, illuminating a well-kept lawn. A row of juniper bushes grew beneath a large bay window. Fireflies blinked in the woods that surrounded the house on three sides.

Amelia brought her father's car to a smooth stop about fifty feet from the curb bordering the front yard.

Parked to the right of the house was a late-model Nissan Pathfinder. Its sleek black body shimmered in the Roadrunner's headlights, as if the vehicle were an animal twitching in its sleep, sensing the presence of danger.

"I'm not sure what I expected," Folline whispered. "It's just so...ordinary?"

"Right?" Cassie agreed.

Amelia killed the ignition and sat there for a minute or two, glaring at the house. She imagined her father feeding sushi to his slut in some fancy restaurant while Mom spooned pudding into the slack mouth of one of her patients. Was he stroking his lover's thigh under the table at this very moment while Mom stole several seconds to massage her aching feet?

She threw open the door, climbed out of the Roadrunner. Her friends followed.

Amelia wasted no time unlocking the trunk. Full dark was upon them, but the nearby streetlamp provided ample lighting for the trio to sort through their arsenal. They had purchased most of their supplies at a local Walmart. Amelia also brought along a baseball bat she had found in the back of her closet, a reminder of when she had played Little League Softball an eternity ago. She thought there might be some sort of devious symbolism in using it for what she had planned tonight—her father was *so* disappointed when she ditched the sport after one season, especially since he had signed on to coach the team—but she didn't put much thought into it. Last but not least was the Punisher knife Folline had borrowed from her brother. It was a slim black blade with a silver skull logo on the hilt. Joey was leaving for boot camp soon, so he probably wouldn't miss it, but Folline made Amelia promise she wouldn't use it to stab anyone.

Amelia had promised. Begrudgingly.

"Alrighty then," she said as she slammed the trunk lid. "Who's ready to teach this goddamn bitch to keep her paws off my dad?"

Once upon a time, her friends would have gasped at hearing such words fall from her lips. Although she was a toddler the last time her family attended church on a regular basis, Amelia was a believer, and as such she usually refrained from using the Lord's name in vain. But a lot had changed these last few weeks. It was as though, to punish her father for his indiscretions, she had abandoned her own values, like a childish hobby she had outgrown along with her innocence.

They walked toward the house, artillery in hand. If this had been an action flick instead of real life, they would have moved in slow motion, three bad-ass chicks accompanied by a bass-heavy hip-hop tune.

Crickets chirped in the roadside foliage like an audience eagerly awaiting a performance for the ages.

A week ago, she had come *this close* to telling Mom.

Dad was working late (supposedly). Mom was downstairs in the living room, watching the news. Amelia had been Snapchatting with Cassie and Folline all evening. Her friends were trying to cheer her up with face filters that transformed them into drooling babies, cartoon animals, and hotties of the opposite sex (the latter sent Amelia into a giggling fit that left her ribs sore, as Folline's male doppelganger was one of the funniest things she had ever seen; they even created a name and background story for him: he was "Colin," a goateed barista who loved hiking and *Game of Thrones*). Around 7:00 p.m. her mother knocked at her bedroom door and suggested they "hang out." Amelia had been avoiding Mom almost as much as she had been avoiding Dad lately, but Mom seemed a little down in the dumps that evening so Amelia figured it was the least she could do.

They spent the next hour or two playing Scrabble at the dining room table, munching on chips and salsa. In the background, on their little breakfast nook TV, gorgeous, golden-skinned couples fell in and out of love on *Bachelor in Paradise*. Now and then Mom made a comment about something on the show ("he should kick her to the curb after what she did with that other guy...if you ask me that tramp is nothing but trouble"), which almost made the whole thing feel like they were buddies the same age instead of mother and daughter. Despite her inner turmoil, Amelia found herself having more fun than she had expected.

Mom won the game with little effort. Amelia enjoyed playing Scrabble, but she would be the first to admit she sucked at it. Adding a hook letter on a triple-word square to turn her daughter's L A D into L A D Y, Mom depleted her remaining tiles with P E R F I D Y.

Amelia challenged it. "That's not a word."

"I beg to differ." Mom flipped through a dictionary. "'*Perfidy. Noun. The quality or state of being faithless or disloyal. Synonyms include unfaithfulness, infideli—*'"

"Got it," Amelia cut her off. "Congratulations. You win."

"Oh, don't be a sore loser. Best two out of three?"

Amelia almost told her everything then. She stared down at P E R F I D Y, wondering if it was a sign from the Man Upstairs. *Do it. Do it* now. *She deserves to know. What are you waiting for?*

Alas, the phone rang as they were clearing the board. Mom got into a lengthy conversation with a co-worker and their rematch was forgotten.

Later that night, Amelia lay awake for hours, staring at the ceiling. Guilt smothered her like an old, dirty blanket crawling with mold and rot. *Why didn't I tell her?* Instead of counting sheep, she counted the reasons why, dismissing them one by one…

What you don't know can't hurt you, went the cliché. *Ignorance is bliss.* But that was bullcrap, wasn't it? Dad's adultery *could* hurt Mom. He might bring home a disease. Amelia had learned about STDs in sex ed class last year. She'd read about what some of them could do to your private parts, and the mental images made her stomach somersault like a drunken gymnast. The rancid details even made Folline a little queasy, she recalled, and Folline lived for gross stuff like that.

Did she, on some subconscious level, wish to protect him because they had always been so close? Amelia was a daddy's girl. And no one was perfect, not even Mom. Maybe their marriage had issues indiscernible to anyone on the outside looking in. Even so, it didn't pardon him of his P E R F I D Y. You were supposed to reconcile with your spouse, not *run off to do the nasty with some floozie.*

Amelia loved her father, but he knew the difference between right and wrong, and he deserved to suffer the consequences of his actions.

Self-preservation, perhaps? She often pondered how different her life would be if her parents split up. Was she doomed to share a bedroom with a half-sibling she despised? *Whatevs.* She knew tons of well-adjusted kids from "broken homes." She recalled feeling a tad envious when her cousin Corey informed her that there was nothing broken about it because you got twice as many presents for Christmas and your birthday. Cassie's folks had both remarried a few years ago, and she adored her "evil stepmother" (they had even gone to a New Kids on the Block reunion show together last summer, and Cassie said she'd never had so much fun).

Truth told, Amelia knew why she had chickened out…

It was simple. The thought of hurting her mother was too much to bear.

He was the one at fault, of course, but she would have been unable to live with herself if she destroyed Mom's world with those five godawful words: *Dad is cheating on you.* Mom worshipped him. She had known since kindergarten that he was destined to be her husband, she had told Amelia on more than one occasion. They had dated off and on throughout high school. He saved her life when she nearly drowned at a pool party the summer after their sophomore year; she returned the favor two years later when he suffered a heat stroke during a pickup basketball game at the park. When they were in college, he wrote a poem about her that was published in a national literary magazine; he used the money for a down payment on her engagement ring. Amelia remembered watching them at a recent barbecue; Mom, tipsy from too many wine coolers, had wrapped her arms around him while he manned the grill, boasting to some friends from down the block about how she felt sorry for them because they would never know what it was like to have the best hubby in the world.

Eventually, Mom would find out how wrong she was about him. Or maybe Dad would see the error of his ways and end the fling on his own. Hopefully sooner than later. And before his junk fell off.

But Amelia couldn't bring herself do it. She didn't think she could ever live with herself if she broke her mother's heart. If finding out from her daughter was the only way, Mom would remain oblivious.

In the meantime, though, she knew she had to do *something*.

As the first rays of the new day's sun slipped into her room the next morning, Amelia typed a quick text to Cassie and Folline so it would be the first thing they saw when they woke up:

> Wut R U2 doin next weekend???
> Think U can sleep over???????

As an afterthought, she added a dozen praying-hand emojis, before climbing out of bed with a craving for pancakes. She thought she might surprise Mom by making breakfast herself. It was the least she could do.

On her way down the hall she passed Dad getting ready for work in the bathroom. Shaving cream covered the bottom half of his face.

"'Morning, pumpkin," he said. "Up before noon? That's gotta be a first."

She replied with a noncommittal grunt.

He chuckled, shook his head. "Teenagers."

This was Amelia's beef. She deserved to throw the first punch. She had something important to say, though, before shit got started. She paced back and forth along the curb at the edge of the front yard, shaking a can of spray paint. The ball bearing inside rattled: *chocka-chocka-chocka.*

A twig snapped in the nearby woods. An owl hooted.

Folline practiced a few cheerleading moves in front of the Roadrunner while they waited: buckets and daggers, low and high "V" motions. The pentagram and skulls on her sleepover wear glowed in the dark like phantasms floating a few feet above the ground. Cassie yawned, fidgeting with her rainbow bracelet as she stared off down the road.

Like soldiers, they both stood at attention when Amelia started talking.

"I don't get it," she said. "They always looked so happy, like they were meant to be together. They have these ridiculous pet names for each other. Sometimes he'll kiss her neck and grab her butt while she's cooking dinner. I tell them to get a room, but I secretly love it. One day I hoped to marry a man who would treat me like Dad treated Mom. Now I know it was a lie. He's willing to throw it all away to rub dicks with some hoochie-mama he met on the Internet."

Folline and Cassie snorted laughter at that last part.

Without further ado, Amelia bent, depressed the nozzle on her can of yellow spray paint, and painted a word on the blacktopped driveway:

She stood back to admire her work.

"Nice," Cassie said.

Amelia dropkicked the empty can. It clattered across the pavement.

"Yo." Cassie reached into one of the shopping bags, tossed a roll of toilet paper at Folline. Then another, and another. "Heads up, ginger Morticia."

Folline caught one, ripped it open. "I always wanted to do this." It's kinda pretty in the end, don't you think? As long as you're not the loser who has to clean it up!"

She pitched a roll into the air. It sailed over the corner of the roof, tumbled to the ground. She sprinted through the grass, picked it up and chucked it in the opposite direction. She yelled for Cassie to give her a hand, and she didn't have to ask twice. Together they draped the eaves and gutters with Great Value Ultra Soft, crisscrossing the yard from one side to the other. They decorated the trees that flanked the front yard, laughing and high-fiving one another as they did so. Their shadows darted back and forth like ghostly co-conspirators beneath the bright white glow of the streetlight.

"Walking in a winter wonderland!" Cassie sang.

Before long, the property was covered in drooping white ribbons, as if a giant spider had wrapped a web around the place with plans to return and drain the life from it later.

While the other two had their fun, Amelia decided those junipers beneath the bay window needed to match the rest of the yard. She emptied a can of white spray paint on the bushes. When that was done, she drew a giant smiley face on the window—a red one, with Xs for eyes and a smile turned upside-down. The paint dripped down the glass and onto the siding like a melting, tormented soul.

She lobbed a brick through the storm door. The crash of shattering glass echoed through the night.

"Oh, snap!" said Cassie.

Amelia surveyed the damage they had done so far, wondering why none of it felt as satisfying as it should have.

By now, Folline and Cassie had depleted their two-ply ammunition. They watched Amelia pick up a new Walmart bag and approach the Pathfinder parked to the right of the house.

"Oh no, she's not," Folline said.

"I think she is," Cassie said.

Amelia tried one of its doors. Locked. She peered through the passenger-side window. A rainbow of bead necklaces, like the kind you got at Mardi Gras for flashing your boobs, dangled from the rearview mirror. Two large black gym bags, a green duffel bag, and a flower-print valise filled the backseat and most of the cargo hold.

She circled the SUV, trailing a finger along its shiny black body. Overhead, moths flitted about the streetlight's softly-humming bulb, like tiny voyeurs watching to see what came next.

Amelia's brow furrowed when she noticed the Pathfinder had an out-of-state tag. Dad's lover was originally from Ohio. That made her pause for a second. She wasn't sure why.

She pried open the door on the gas tank and screwed off the lid. Ripped a hole in a four-pound bag of sugar.

Her friends strolled over to watch. Folline was carrying the Louisville Slugger, pretending it was a guitar.

The sugar slid into the tank with a whisper.

"Take it all," Amelia said. "Yeahhh…you like that, don't you?"

"Oh, you are vicious!" Cassie said.

"Hope he was worth it," Folline said.

Amelia dropped the empty bag, dusted off her palms. "That felt good. But I wanna go inside now."

Folline gave her the bat.

"*Gracias.*" Amelia strutted across the yard as if she'd been sent in to pinch-hit for the Braves. Scratch that—her father loved the Braves. He'd taken her to see a game when she was eight or nine, a father-daughter daytrip to Atlanta back when things were hunky-dory. She imagined she wore a Mets uniform instead.

She climbed the curved brick steps, opened the storm door. Pieces of broken glass fell from its busted window with an almost musical tinkle, crunching beneath her sneakers.

"Careful," Folline said.

"Who's got the knife?" Amelia said. "I wonder if I can pick the lo—"

She gripped the doorknob. Turned it.

The door swung open.

"Ummm...okay." She glanced back at her friends. "I didn't expect *that*."

"Whoa," Folline and Cassie said at the same time.

"So excited for her 'romantic weekend' she forgot to lock up, I guess."

Amelia tightened her grip on the bat. Stepped into the house.

Folline and Cassie shared an uneasy look before following her inside.

Last night her father had knocked at her bedroom door. Tentatively. As if he could read her mind and knew she would have preferred to see anyone else standing there: Donald Trump...Hitler...Pennywise the clown...even her archenemy, Jennifer Mebane, might have been more welcome (Jennifer was a loudmouthed gossip who almost had everyone in their eighth-grade class believing Amelia, Folline, and Cassie were three sides of a lesbian love triangle).

"You're still awake," Dad said.

"It's only nine o' clock," Amelia said.

"Permission to enter?"

When she didn't respond, he stepped into her room anyway. He wore plaid pajama bottoms and smelled like Old Spice. His hair was wet and looked blacker than ever. Amelia had heard him brag to Mom about how most of his peers were almost fully gray, but at forty-three years old he had yet to find a single silver hair on his body. Judging from his rapidly-receding hairline, though, Brian Fletcher would be completely bald before he was fifty. Maybe he shouldn't be so boastful about the fruit on his tree when his branches would soon go bare.

Before he interrupted, she'd been sitting up in bed, researching the psychology of infidelity on her laptop: *25% of married men admit they have cheated on their wives...over 50% of those unfaithful husbands claim to be happy at home...only 15% of marriages tarnished by an affair ultimately end in divorce.* Nothing she had learned made her feel any better. Her family was another sorry statistic.

She closed the Chromebook, set it aside. "You need something?"

"I got to thinking about how I used to tuck you in when you were little," he said.

"Long time ago," she said.

"Not that long ago."

She shrugged.

"Early flight tomorrow," he said. "Thought I'd come say goodnight, tell you I love you in case you're still snoozing when I take off."

"Goodnight," she said.

"Amelia, is something wrong?"

"Why would you think something's wrong?"

He crossed the room, sat beside her on the edge of her bed.

"It's just...I can't help feeling like I'm *persona non grata* around here lately. If I didn't know better, I'd think you've been avoiding me." He sniffed at his armpits, chuckled. "Do I stink or something?"

"You don't stink," she said.

Actually, he smelled nice. As far back as she could remember, she had adored her father's scent. It was the smell of strength. Security. *Goodness.* But so much had changed.

"What is it then, sweetheart? What's going on with you?"

"Nothing's going on with *me*."

He glanced around her room, as if seeing everything for the first time: the dog-eared copy of *Thirteen Reasons Why* on her nightstand, the life-size poster of her favorite female boxer ("FIGHT LIKE A GIRL!") taped to her closet door, Bradley and Gaga in their aquarium atop her dresser, and the jars of makeup and perfume cluttering the surface of her vanity. When his gaze fell upon a pair of her panties lying atop the laundry hamper, he quickly looked down at his bedroom slippers.

She stared at a spot on his neck where she could see his pulse beating beneath his skin. Imagined the other woman kissing him there, running her hands through his hair. *Gross.*...

"So, um, your friends are sleeping over this weekend?" he asked her.

"Yep."

"Sounds fun. I'll leave you some cash. You can order pizzas. Watch Netflix and chill."

"That doesn't mean what you think it means."

"No?"

"You should Google it. I'm not gonna explain it to you."

"Fair enough. Maybe I will." He stood with a defeated sigh. "I'll get out of your hair. If you're sure there's nothing we need to talk about."

"Dad?"

"Yeah?"

"What did you think about Tyler?"

"Tyler? He's okay. Doesn't strike me as the brightest bulb in the chandelier, but if he treats you right that's all I care about. I haven't seen him around lately. Are you two still—"

"We broke up two weeks ago. Tyler's a cheating d-bag."

Dad blinked at her. The aquarium *bloop*ed on the other side of the room.

She yawned, grabbed her iPhone off the nightstand. "I wanna go to bed now. Close the door on your way out, please?"

Her thumbs moved at superhuman speed as she rattled off a group text to Folline and Cassie:

OMG I can't even.....my dad walks around actin like everything's perfect but he's so DEAD to me!!!!

Her father's lips parted as if he were about to say something else. But he must have decided against it. He cleared his throat and nodded before leaving the room.

After fumbling around in the dark for a few seconds, Amelia found a light switch. She flicked it on.

"Oh, crap," Folline said. "I just thought of something. Gloves! We should've worn gloves. Our fingerprints are gonna be everywhere!"

"That *just now* occurred to you?" Cassie said.

"I can't remember everything."

"You're supposed to be the expert on this stuff. Hope you remember to check for a pulse first when you're cutting people open for a living one day!"

"You're *sooo* funny."

"I couldn't care less about fingerprints," Amelia said. "What's she gonna do, turn us in? Cheating's a felony in some states. Mom could sue this piece of trash for everything she's worth and she would totally win. It's called 'alienation of affection.'"

"No kidding?" said Cassie.

"No kidding. Jeez Louise, this place is fifty shades of *fugly*."

The walls were mustard yellow. The carpet was the color of dried blood. A hideous brown sofa sat against the back wall, behind an oval-shaped coffee table. A floor lamp in one corner gave off a sickly orange glow. To the right of the living room, beyond a curved archway, was a kitchen and dining area with a green tile floor; to the left was a dark hallway. The air had a slightly stale odor.

No photos adorned the walls, nothing to give the place any hint of personality. In fact, several items scattered atop the coffee table were the only clue that anyone lived here at all: a wine cooler bottle with a few sips left in the bottom, a legal pad, a pink vaping mod, and a laptop computer. The laptop was open but its power was off.

Amelia picked up the notepad. Three lines were scribbled in blue ink on the first page:

$90/week

770-555-8745

"Meel?" Cassie said. "What's on your mind, girl?"

Amelia chewed at her bottom lip, couldn't put into words what was bothering her. She only knew something didn't feel right. Not that there was anything *right* about this whole sordid mess. But it was more than her father's infidelity. Something *else* was going on here. An ominous feeling nagged at the back of her brain, like a finger jabbing at the soft tissue without poking all the way through: *The license plate from the Buckeye State…the bags in the back of the Pathfinder…the unlocked front door…and now this note…what does it all mean?* Inexplicably, she was reminded of a boardgame her parents had purchased at a yard sale when she was nine or ten. The pieces were all there, but when they sat down to play as a family no one could figure out the objective since the instructions were missing. Amelia never enjoyed winning as much as she should have after they made up their own rules. No victory felt 100% legit. Truth told, she didn't like playing the game at all because the whole thing felt like…cheating.

In the books she read, people were always scratching their heads when they were puzzled by something. She had never seen anyone do that in real life. But she did it now. She couldn't shake the suspicion that there was something more sinister going on here than just some sleazy affair. What was it, though?

She flung the pad across the room, stared down at the laptop. Stuck to its lid were two monochrome decals. One advertised a rock band called Optic Oppression. The other was Buffalo Bill primping in front of the mirror in *The Silence of the Lambs* ("I'D FUCK ME").

Amelia poked at the laptop with the end of her Louisville Slugger, as if the Lenovo ThinkPad were some venomous creature she had stumbled upon and she needed to confirm if it was dead or only sleeping. She wondered if it had all started *right here.* She imagined Dad's mistress spread out on her ugly couch, wearing yoga pants that showed her nasty camel-toe, sipping Jamaican Me Happy wine coolers and puffing on the end of her stupid vape thing while she searched Facebook for something *else* to puff on…

With a murderous scream, she brought the bat down on the computer. Her first blow cracked its housing. But she didn't stop there. She hit it again and again, attacking the machine as if it were the cause of all the world's problems. Pieces of shattered plastic and twisted metal flew into the air. Number and letter keys rattled across the surface of the coffee table like broken fingerbones.

"*Mom has some LEFTOVERS in the FRIDGE! You want those TOO?*" she shrieked, emphasizing every third or fourth word with another strike of the bat. "*A MARRIAGE is between TWO people, but SOME bitches NEVER learned how to COUNT!*"

Before long the computer's guts were exposed, and she destroyed those too: its motherboard brain shot through with copper veins, its nervous system of capacitors, resistors, connectors, and ports, and its round black battery heart. A sliver of green plastic leapt up and scratched the tip of her nose as if the laptop made one final, futile gesture to defend itself. A memory module got tangled in her hair like a silver bug in search of blood.

At last, she dropped the bat. It *clunk*ed onto the floor.

"Holy crap," Folline said.

Cassie said: "That. Was. *Awesome.*"

Breathing heavily, Amelia asked, "Who's got the paint?"

Cassie reached into a shopping bag. "We've got...black and red left. Whatcha want?"

"I don't care."

Cassie tossed her a can.

Amelia shook it: *chocka-chocka-chocka*. She jumped up onto the couch. Ancient springs squeaked in protest. She depressed the nozzle and the can hissed like a spitting serpent as she scrawled a warning across the rear wall of the living room:

"Whoa," Folline said. "That's pretty specific... "

"And?" Amelia hopped off the couch. "We're sending a message here. She's gotta know she's bumped uglies with my dad for the last time. See ya, wouldn't wanna be ya, move on to the next unfaithful husband 'cause this one's off limits, rotten-crotch."

"You kiss your Mom with that mouth?" asked Cassie.

"Don't be jealous."

Folline stepped into the dark kitchen/dining room adjacent to the den. She swept a bowl of plastic fruit off a scuffed tabletop and its contents rolled across the floor. She kicked a fake apple over to Cassie. Cassie lobbed it back, then struck a victorious pose like Megan Rapinoe after her team's gold-medal win at the World Cup finals. Folline doubled over with laughter.

"Yo, C-Mac," Amelia said. "You're the artist. You should paint us a pretty picture."

"*Moi?*" Cassie said.

They started chanting her name.

Cassie made a face as if considering her options, taking a moment to find her inspiration…

…before painting a big black dick on the wall beside the front door.

"I think it might be your best work yet," Amelia said when it was done.

"It's a masterpiece," Folline said. "It should be in the Louvre."

Cassie took a bow.

"Let's see what else we can get into," Amelia said, strutting out of the living room and down a hallway that led toward the back of the house. "Somebody bring the rest of the stuff, 'cause I'm just getting started."

Amelia strolled down the hall, her friends following behind her but not too closely. She held the Punisher knife in an overhanded grip. The blade scraped along the wall with a sound like an old man's snore, gouging into the tacky brown and yellow wallpaper. The design depicted plump owls perched on gnarled tree limbs. Every few feet she paused to blind one of the birds, stabbing out its eyes while she fantasized about what she might do if granted five minutes alone with Dad's mistress.

The other two couldn't stop giggling over Cassie's work of art. Folline asked Cassie how she knew what a penis looked like, and Cassie said she had learned all she ever wanted to know from a book she had at home: *Drawing Human Anatomy*. She used it when she worked on her comics. There were tons of penises in its pages.

"Penises? Penisi? What's the plural of 'penis?'"

"I'm pretty sure it's just penises."

The desecrated walls vibrated with their laughter.

They passed a laundry closet (Amelia stopped to paint "F" and "U" on the washer and dryer with a new can of paint)...a bathroom that stank of mildew...and a bedroom with walls covered in faded wood paneling (it was empty except for a dog's chew toy, shaped like an alligator, lying in one corner). Then—

Amelia froze. Folline and Cassie slammed into her from behind.

Ahead, at the end of the hall, was what they assumed to be the master bedroom. Its door hung ajar.

"There's a light on in there," Amelia said. "Why is there a light on in there?"

"You said nobody was home," Folline said. "I thought she went with your dad."

"She did," Amelia said.

"But what if you're wrong?" asked Cassie.

"If I was wrong, she would have come out by now."

"Can't argue with that," Folline said.

Amelia took a deep breath. Wished she hadn't left the baseball bat in the other room.

She stepped forward, pushed on the door. It swung open with a whisper on shag carpet.

The room reeked of perfume and—although none of the girls possessed the life experience to identify such a smell – the musky odor of sex. Several blankets lay crumpled on the floor, between a queen-sized bed and a closet with no door. Atop a nightstand, next to a gaudy green lamp with a rust-colored shade, lay a tube of K-Y jelly and something else unfamiliar to Amelia and her friends: a cock ring. It was neon blue, with a two-pronged bullet-shaped contraption on top, like some extraterrestrial wedding band. A dresser sat against one wall. Behind a yellow curtain, a window looked out on the thick black night. Adjacent to the master bedroom was a brightly-lit bathroom; a bottle of women's shaving gel and a pink razor were visible through its open doorway, sitting on the side of the tub.

In the far corner of the room, attached to a tripod, was an expensive-looking video camera.

Cassie approached the camera, peered through its viewfinder. "Looks like she's a regular white-trash Kathryn Bigelow."

"Who dat?" asked Folline.

"*Zero Dark Thirty*? *The Hurt Locker*? Hello! *Near Dark*, one of the best vampire movies ever made? She's only an Oscar-winning director! Do you watch *anything* besides true crime documentaries?"

"Cheerleading competitions on YouTube," Folline said.

"You are hopeless."

Amelia stalked across the room, kicked the crumpled blankets out of her way and started rifling through the closet. Wire hangers rattled like bratty children attempting to get the last word. She didn't find much. A sheer burgundy blouse. A pair of ladies' jeans. A leopard-print bra. And...a purple silk shirt and khaki shorts? She paused. Those last two articles of clothing looked like menswear. She yanked the blouse off its hanger, whirled around and threw it on the bed.

"Check it out. Chanel. Miss Thang is *fancy*. Somebody pass the bleach over here, stat. She won't wear this again."

"Coming right up." The jug sloshed in Cassie's grip as she pulled it out of a bag and brought it over.

"I almost can't watch," said Folline. "Hey...what's that?"

A thick book bound in red faux leather sat atop the nearby dresser, beneath a Polaroid camera, the kind with a flashbulb on top.

Cassie shoved the camera aside, picked up the book. "A photo album?"

"Great," Amelia said. "I can't wait to see all of her precious memories."

"Curiosity killed the cat." Cassie sat on the edge of the bed with the book balanced on her thighs.

"Who even uses these anymore?" Folline said, examining the bulky camera like an archaeologist inspecting some ancient artifact.

She peered through the viewfinder, pointed the camera at Amelia. "Say cheese."

"Don't you dare."

"Just kidding." Folline put the camera back where she got it, plopped down on the bed beside Cassie. "Scooch."

Cassie opened the album to the first page.

Folline said, "Uhhh…"

"Yo, Meel," Cassie said. "You might wanna peep this, girl."

"Can't you see I'm busy?" Amelia grunted, straining to get the safety cap off the Clorox jug.

"Get your butt over here."

Amelia set the jug down near the video camera tripod. She joined Folline and Cassie on the edge of the bed.

The first photo in the album appeared to have been taken several years ago, as Dad's lover looked younger here than in the pictures Amelia had seen on his phone. Her hair was longer, and she might have been ten pounds heavier. She wore a wedding dress with a long, flowing train. Her groom was an athletic-looking man in a light blue tuxedo, with shoulder-length brown hair. The couple stood hand in hand before a chubby minister.

Cassie said, "Shut the front door. She's *married?*"

"Looks like it," Folline said. "Ah-oh…"

Amelia blinked down at the book.

Cassie turned the page.

The next photo was a more recent shot of the happy couple. A blown-up portrait from a photo booth. The man faced the camera, one corner of his mouth turned up in a cocky smirk. His eyes were a bright, almost supernatural blue. Except for the frosted bangs that framed his face, his hair was cut short here and spiked with some sort of gel. His wife's lips were pursed in a classic "duckface" expression. Specks of glitter glistened on her cheeks and in her hair. Her hand was on his throat. Her nails were the same color as his eyes.

"Dang," Folline said. "Hubby's kinda yummy."

Cassie shot her a look: *Seriously?*

"Just saying. A girl would have to be *cray-cray* to cheat on him."
Cassie pinched Folline's arm.

"Ow. Sorry, Meel. I didn't mean that the way it sounded. Your dad, he's handsome enough, but—"

"Quit while you're ahead," Cassie said.

Folline mimed zipping her lips shut.

Cassie said something about how the guy kinda looked like Patrick Wilson, that dude from *The Conjuring* and *Insidious*. Murmurs of agreement. They had watched those movies during a sleepover at Folline's place last Halloween and subsequently stayed up all night trying to scare the crap out of each other.

"Oh, snap!" Folline said. "We should tell him what his wife's been up to! We could *ruin* her nasty ass."

Cassie said, "Oh, let's do that."

"Wait," Amelia said. "Lemme see that?"

Cassie handed her the album. Amelia flipped through its pages. The clear film protecting the photos made a crinkling noise.

The girls' eyes grew wide when they saw what else was in there.

"Oh my," Cassie gasped, covered her mouth with one hand.

Folline said, "That ain't no acorn."

The rest of the album was filled with snapshots of memories the couple had shared through the years, but none were the saccharine stuff Amelia and her friends expected to see: the sweethearts lounging on a sunlit beach, sipping at strawberry daquiris; or shrouded in fog at a costume party, his plastic fangs bared for the camera as she feigned terror, the "holes" in her neck oozing "blood"; or dressed to kill for a night on the town, Mrs. Sleazebag displaying enough cleavage to make other men's heads turn while the Patrick Wilson lookalike wore his sunglasses after dark because you *know* he was the type. No, beyond those first two innocuous pages were glossy images of a more licentious nature...

Hubby's standing nude before an olive-skinned woman wearing only a peach-colored bra. His hands are tangled in her messy black hair. Her face is buried between his legs...

Wifey's in bed with a long-haired man whose hands are cuffed to the headboard. She pinches her nipples, her head thrown back in ecstasy, as she rides him like a cowgirl...

Here's her husband again, doing it "doggy-style" with a chubby blonde. Massive gold hoops dangle from her ears. He's flashing a wide, white grin, giving a thumbs-up to the camera as he takes her from behind...

Here's his better half, beneath a skinny hipster type with a beard and lots of tattoos. He's still wearing his knee-high socks as he plows into her. Her teeth are bared, giving her a vicious, feral look as her nails rake down his back...

Hubby, buttocks dimpled, atop a big-breasted redhead...

Wifey, sitting on the face of a muscular twentysomething...

Each of the shots was part of a set. Each set was compiled of no less than a dozen images featuring one of the couple engaged in sexual acts with an extramarital lover. Every set was labelled with a small card, on which a single name was written in black Sharpie: the woman in the peach-colored bra was NADINE. LIAM was the long-haired guy. The chubby blonde was JANICE. RICHARD was the hipster. SHAUNA, CHAD, and so on. Judging from the thickness of the album there were many other names, more unwitting stars of amateur kink shot for the couple's private collection. All of the photos appeared to have been snapped covertly, as if through a window or a crack in a door. They painted a portrait of two people with a proclivity for polygamy, voyeurism, and God knew what else.

The girls stared at each other, red-faced.

"Oh, gag," said Folline. "Would you look at that?"

Cassie tilted her head to view the page from another angle. "Is he—"

"He's licking her butthole," Folline confirmed.

Although her first instinct was to titter along with her friends at the sight of so many exposed private parts and the things adults did with them behind closed doors, Amelia could not forget that her own father was a part of this. He had become the latest addition to their collection, she was sure, and if the photos were in chronological order, she would discover any second now that BRIAN was in here with the rest of—

She threw the album back into Cassie's lap, wiped her hands on the mattress as if she had touched something slimy. "I don't wanna see anymore. If this is some blackmail thing, I don't even care. That's his problem. All I know is, I've seen enough, and we should go now."

"Yeah," Cassie said. "This is seriously effed up. Come on. Let's—"

"—make like a fetus and head out," Folline said.

"I was gonna say let's roll, but you always make it gross."

"It was gross before I got here, dude."

Amelia said, "Quit joking around, you two. Let's get out of here. Like, *yesterday*."

But as Cassie stood, the album dropped from her lap...

...and fell open to a picture of a slack-jawed man with unfocused, bloodshot eyes. A man who, at first glance, appeared to be blackout drunk.

Folline rose to her feet, did a little step-touch dance move. But when she glanced down at the man in the photo, she said, "What the hell?"

She instantly went pale.

"What?" said Amelia.

"It's the long-haired dude. The one handcuffed to the bed."

"Lemme guess, he's super tasty and you wanna have his babies," Cassie said, already moving across the room. She came back for Folline, grabbed her by the arm. "Meel's right. We gotta move."

"What about him, Folline?" asked Amelia.

Folline continued to stare down at the photo. "He...no, that can't be right."

"Earth to the rest of my crew," Cassie said. "Unless you pervs are planning to hang around for your own lovefest with these freaky-deaks, I suggest we—"

"Hold on a second, Cassie!" Amelia snapped at her. "Folline, what is it? What's wrong?"

"Look at his eyes," Folline said, with a tremor in her voice.

"What about them?"

"See how they're filled up with blood? That looks like subconjunctival hemorrhaging. And those dark patches? They call that 'racoon eyes.' It happens when there's blunt force trauma to the head."

Amelia stared at her. "What are you trying to say?"

"You guys...I think that man is *dead*."

"Give me a break!" Cassie said. "This is really not the time, ginger Morticia."

Folline fell to her knees beside the photo album. Her long red hair swayed back and forth as she turned the pages. "Oh, God. Look. Look! Do you believe me now?"

The tattooed hipster stands shirtless in the foreground, his mouth a shocked "O" as a splash of crimson spurts from his forehead. Behind him, wearing nothing but a cloak of shadows, stands the Patrick Wilson clone. He's pointing a small handgun at the back of the hipster's head...

Cassie joined her friends on the floor. Turned to another page.

The chubby blonde with the gold hoop earrings is on her hands and knees again, but this time her lips are blue and her eyes are bugging out of her head. She's clawing at her throat as Brian Fletcher's mistress strangles her from behind with a belt...

"Umm...Meel?" Cassie said. "What have you gotten us into here?"

"I don't know."

Folline flipped forward a few more pages. Her mouth hung open as she studied the grisly images in front of her, as if she were simultaneously horrified and mesmerized.

The homewrecker sits nude in a recliner, her legs spread, and once again the twentysomething's head is positioned between her thighs. But this time it is only his head. He has been decapitated. He gawks at the camera, his tongue lolling out one side of his mouth, while the woman licks blood off her fingers…

The girls sprang to their feet at the same time. Cassie kicked the album across the room.

"Holy shit, I've read about this!" Folline said. "It's rare, but sometimes they work in pairs. Like the Lonely Hearts Killers, back in the '40s? Or Paul and Karla, those scumbags up in Canada? Ian Brady and Myra Hindley used to get off on reading about Nazi atrocities together when they weren't snapping selfies by their victims' gravesites. Not that selfies were a thing back then, but you know what I—"

"OMG!" Cassie said. "Nobody is impressed with your serial killer trivia, weirdo!"

"It's some kind of sick game they play. They cheat while the other one watches, and after they've had their fun, they murder the—"

"Affair partner," Amelia finished for her, recalling the phrase from her research on infidelity. She hated it, as those two words implied something neat, clean, a collaboration between two co-workers assigned to the same platonic task. Calling Dad's slut-puppy his *affair partner* was like calling a hurricane that claimed hundreds of lives "a spot of bad weather."

Her heart leapt into her throat. "Oh, God…he's with her right now! I have to warn him before it's too late!"

Amelia dug through the pockets of her PJs. Found her iPhone. She unlocked it, swiped through her contacts until she found DAD. She held the phone to her ear.

All the anger she had bottled up inside these last few weeks, all the disgust she had felt for him every time she saw his face…suddenly, none of it mattered. He had made a terrible mistake, but she loved him. Even if he was a lying cheat, he was still her *daddy.*

"Pick up. Please pick up!" Her voice was a pitiful whine.

"You can do that on the way. Let's go." Cassie pulled her friends toward the door.

"Wait," Folline said. "Do you guys hear that?"

Everyone froze. For the next few seconds, none of the girls dared to even breathe.

From somewhere on the opposite end of the house: the recorded sound of an electric guitar.

Although she was no fan of old-fogey music like Guns n' Roses, Amelia did think it was kinda neat when Dad had programmed his new phone to play the intro to their most famous song any time he got a call from his daughter ("'Sweet Child o' Mine'," he had said with a goofy grin, "See what I did there?").

Now that eight-bar melody was the most bone-chilling sound she had ever heard.

It was scarier than the midnight click-and-sigh of her closet door swinging open when she was five, when she was convinced that a tentacled thing with a hunger for little girls lurked inside there. It was more ominous than when her beloved Biscuit had gone missing several years ago, and she overheard a neighbor telling Mom she was pretty sure she had seen the poodle lying in a ditch at the end of their block.

Folline obviously recognized the song too. It had been the soundtrack to one of her team's most complicated cheer routines last year. "Amelia," she whispered, "isn't that…"

"Y-yeah."

The temperature in the room seemed to plummet as they all realized what was happening.

The music grew louder. Closer. It was in the hallway now. Right outside the bedroom. With it came the creak of a floorboard. Footsteps.

Goosebumps prickled Amelia's forearms. "Dad…?"

One-half of the demented duo from the photo album stepped into the room. The handsome husband.

Amelia recognized the phone in his hand right away. Its case was printed with the Atlanta Braves' "tomahawk" logo. Her father's Samsung. She dropped her iPhone. It bounced off her foot and thumped on the floor.

The man tapped REJECT CALL and said with a sneer, "Sorry. He can't talk right now."

He wore a tight blue Under Armour T-shirt, black jogging shorts, and gray Nikes with yellow laces. He was shorter in person than he had appeared in the photos. His face and arms were shiny with sweat as if he had just completed a rigorous fitness regimen. He had the most intense blue eyes any of the girls had ever seen, like sparkling sapphires set within his skull. His voice held the slightest hint of a Southern accent.

"I've gotta say...I love what you've done with the place."

"There's three of us and one of him," Cassie said. "Run."

The man slid Brian Fletcher's cell phone into a pocket of his jogging shorts. "If I were you, I wouldn't move a goddamn muscle."

"Or what?" Cassie said, holding her arms out to the side to protect her buddies behind her.

"Trust me. You'll regret it if you do." The man whistled through his teeth, said something that sounded like German: "*Hier.*"

A dog padded into the room behind him, a slender Doberman Pinscher with fur as black as sin. It wore a collar studded with rubies, like drops of blood shimmering in the overhead light. Its eyes were the color of an old rusty blade. In the still, quiet room, the sound its claws made on the thick shag carpet was like a madman picking at scabs, lifting and pulling away, lifting and pulling away. Otherwise the animal made no sound at all until its master gave his command.

"Her name's Delilah. Say hello, Delilah."

The dog barked once in the girls' direction.

They flinched.

The man scratched the dog behind her ears. A low growl rumbled in the Doberman's throat, as if to warn Amelia and her friends: *One wrong move and you're dead. I'll do anything for him. All he has to do is say the word...*

"We didn't see anything," Folline said, her bottom lip quivering. "Honestly, we didn't."

"Nice try, but I don't believe that, Red." He glanced over at the photo album. It laid against the wall, open but facedown where Cassie had kicked it, like a bird felled by a hunter's bullet. "At this point, I'll bet you've seen *everything*."

He picked up the album. Brushed it off. Sat it down on a nearby nightstand.

"Please," Amelia said. "Let us go."

"Did you *like* what you saw?"

The girls held one another.

"It's sad, really. Guy can't even go for a moonlight jog without returning to discover three juvenile delinquents have trashed everything in sight."

Cassie stepped back, still gripping Amelia and Folline each by an arm. They all watched the dog. The dog watched them back. When Cassie's calves collided with the bed, she sat, pulling her friends down with her like marionettes whose strings had been snipped.

"You girls have no idea what you've stumbled into," said the man.

The dog barked a short, sharp amen.

"*Sitz.*"

Delilah sat, and for the next few minutes she was as still as a statue carved from the night itself. Her tall, slender ears stood at attention.

The man bent, helped himself to Amelia's phone. "Who else has one of these? Give it up."

"I don't have a phone," Cassie said. "I dropped mine in the bathtub."

"I don't have one either," Folline said.

"You must think I'm stupid. You're, what—fifteen, sixteen? I doubt you could change your tampons without posting about it on TikTok."

The dog made a snuffling noise, as if snickering at her master's crude joke.

"I'm not gonna ask you again." The man snapped his fingers. His nails were well-manicured. He wore a silver wedding band with a black gem set in the middle of it.

Scowling, Folline reached into her T-shirt. She pulled her iPhone out of her bra and slapped it into his palm.

He sniffed it. Grinned. Dropped it into his pocket. "That's what I thought." He stared at her for longer than was necessary. "You got a name, Red? I can't just call you Red all night."

"Folline." She squirmed beneath his gaze.

"Come again?"

"My name is Folline."

"What kinda name is Folline?" He reached out, stroked her chin with the tip of one finger. "Are you some kind of fallen angel? You look like you might be."

She recoiled.

Delilah whined, as if jealous of the attention her master was affording these human females.

He held his empty hand out toward Cassie. "Next."

Cassie crossed her arms in front of her chest.

"Still going with 'I dropped it in the tub?'"

"I am, because that's what happened."

"Fine. What's your name?"

"Peter Parker."

"Tough guy, huh? Good thing we've got pics, and I'm in a playful mood."

He glanced down at the screen of Amelia's iPhone, scrolled through her contacts. After only a few seconds, he turned the phone to show the girls what he found. It was a photo of Cassie, taken on "Hippie Day" during Prep Week last year. She wore a tie-dyed headband and John Lennon sunglasses.

"Nice to meet you…CASSIE."

He tapped her contact, then SPEAKER. It went straight to voicemail: "Yo. This is C-Mac. I can't take your call right now, but leave a message and I'll hit you back if I feel like it!"

He hung up. "Guess you were telling the truth." Amelia's iPhone disappeared into his pocket. "What were you doing with your phone in the tub? That's what I wanna know."

He winked at her.

Cassie replied with an expression that said, *You're a pig.*

"And we already know you're AMELIA. Ask me, it doesn't fit you at all. Sounds like an old woman's name."

"Good thing nobody asked you," Amelia shot back. She was, in fact, named after her maternal grandmother. But she would eat one of his Doberman's turds before she volunteered such personal info to this creep.

"Salty," said the man. "I like you."

Footsteps from down the hallway then. A shadow slid into the room ahead of its owner.

Both man and dog turned toward the door. Delilah barked a hello a second before her master said, "Look who's here. Nice of you to join us."

"Hiya, handsome. Where have you been all my life?"

Amelia's hands balled into fists. Her nostrils flared. Cassie and Folline each grabbed her by one arm as the woman stepped into the room.

It was *her.* Dad's mistress. She wore tight blue leggings, green running shoes, and a T-shirt that read "SEE NO EVIL" beneath a grainy image of a goth girl with her eyes scratched out. Her hair was tied back in a bun at the nape of her neck. She was sweaty like her husband. In one hand she gripped a water bottle; the other held the pink vaping mod that had been sitting on the table beside the laptop Amelia destroyed. She sucked on the end of the device, exhaled a cloud of white smoke that filled the room with a cotton candy aroma.

"What took you so long?" the man asked her. "Never used to beat you back. Slowing down in your old age?"

"Shut your mouth."

"Am I gonna have to trade you in for a younger model? Maybe one who doesn't smoke?"

"You do it, you die." She handed him the water bottle, glanced at a Fitbit strapped to her left wrist before leaning down to make kissy-faces at the Doberman, scratching the top of the dog's head with one long, pink-nailed finger. Where her husband spoke with a slight Southern accent, she could have come from anywhere. "Sometimes a girl likes to stop and smell the roses. I always thought you could smell them best at night, when they don't have to compete with all the other smells in the world. Cars, people...prepubescent troublemakers armed with paint and toilet paper."

"You're weird."

"It's why you fell in love with me."

"It's one reason."

"Anywho...I thought we didn't keep secrets from each other, Dom. If I had known we were having guests tonight I would have straightened up a bit."

The man chuckled, took a swig from the water bottle. "Surprise. We've got ourselves a party, baby."

The woman crossed the room, stood over the photo album sitting on the nightstand. She stroked its cover almost lovingly. "This has been moved. I'm assuming they know about us?"

"Yeah, they know."

"They sure did a number on the house. I'm almost impressed."

"Guess we can kiss our deposit goodbye."

The woman held a hand to her chest, as if in great distress. "Whatever will we do?"

"Old fart'll probably stroke out when he sees the damage they've done. Serves him right, the way he kept ogling your tits that day."

"Stop. He was harmless."

"Pretty funny if you think about it. An hour from now we would have been long gone. These three dumbasses must have the worst luck on Earth."

Suddenly, Amelia understood what had been nagging at the back of her brain since they first started breaking bad on this place. It all became clear, like frost on a windshield dissipating in the heat of the morning sun. Five years ago she had spent a week with an aunt and uncle who owned a trailer park. They had been remodeling one of their ancient mobile homes during her stay. Amelia remembered the cheap, dated furniture, faded wallpaper, gaudy wood paneling, and the stale odor that permeated every room. It didn't matter to the people who rented from Aunt Eileen and Uncle Freddy, though. Fancy décor wasn't something their tenants required, because their stay was temporary. They were always just passing through, from one place to another...

"For the record," said the homewrecker, "I am super-pissed about my laptop. Little cunts murdered it."

"I'll buy you another one, baby."

"You're sweet."

"I'm pretty sure they also put sugar in our gas tank."

"Ouch."

"Good thing is, they brought something in trade."

"The Roadrunner? I saw it. Goddamn, that thing is sexy."

"Don't fall in love with it. You know we'll have to ditch it in a day or two. A ride like that, it'll draw too much attention."

The woman made a pouty face.

Like the rental property, Amelia realized now that the out-of-state license plate on the Pathfinder made perfect sense as well. These two deviants probably owned a whole stack of them, frequently switching out the tags like the fugitives always did on Folline's true crime shows. They were drifters. Nomads. It explained the note on the coffee table too. They were already preparing to move on, to rent another home where they could start their twisted game all over again.

"So, do these wannabe thugs have names?"

"Oh, how rude of me. Honey...meet Folline, Cassie, and Amelia. Teenyboppers, this is my lovely wife, Petra."

"Charmed, I'm sure. He's Dominick. Let's talk about the elephant in the room. Which one of you belongs to Brian?"

When she got no reply, the woman named Petra cocked her hip and took another long pull from her vaping mod. She looked the girls up and down, one by one.

Dominick leered at Folline behind his wife's back. Licked his lips. Folline stared down at the skulls on her pajamas.

The sweet scent of cotton candy filled the room again. Three smoke rings shimmied through the air toward Amelia like a tractor beam in a cheesy sci-fi flick.

"It's you, isn't it?"

Amelia glared at her, biting her bottom lip almost hard enough to draw blood.

"I know it's you." Petra grinned like a predator toying with her prey, flashing perfect white teeth. She leaned down in Amelia's face. Up close she smelled like sweat and talcum powder. "I can see the resemblance. Not to mention, you look like you would sell your soul right now to claw my fucking eyes out."

"You are so right about that," Amelia said.

"Hmm," said Petra.

"By the way, I thought it was Zoe." Amelia spat out that last word, the name the temptress had used when flirting with Dad online, as if it were obscene.

"Sometimes. Other times it's not."

"Where is he? Did you...hurt him?"

"Dom," Petra said, "She wants to know what we did with her father."

"Yeahhh. About that..."

Petra walked over to the photo album on the nightstand. Flipped through it. "Guess they didn't finish the book. Too bad. The last chapter is the best part."

"Oh, God," Amelia said.

"Of course, it *is* a work in progress." She winked at her husband.

"I prefer the movie version," Dominick said.

His wife threw back her head, let out a husky, almost masculine laugh.

Dominick said, "Petra, she's old school. When we first met, swear to God, she had a shoebox full of those old funeral photos. Like the ones they used to take in Victorian times—"

"Death portraits," Folline said.

Cassie jabbed her in the side with an elbow.

"I thought it was strange back then, but...well, ya know."

"We all have our 'thing,'" Petra said. "He came around."

"Tell me what you did to him," Amelia said through clenched teeth.

An exasperated sigh. "Dom, I guess we have to spell it out for her because she's dumber than she looks. Take a peek outside, daddy's girl. All of your questions will be answered."

"What?" said Amelia. "I don't—"

"You heard me. Walk to the window. And look outside."

Amelia couldn't move. Every drop of blood in her veins had turned to ice. "Why? What's out there?"

Dominick's hands gripped Petra's waist. He waggled his eyebrows at Amelia. "Go on. Take a look."

"Sometime this century, sugar. We're already behind schedule, thanks to you."

Amelia rose from the bed.

The dog stood too, barked a warning at her.

"*Nein*, Delilah," Dominick said.

The dog made a snuffling noise again. She maintained her position, but the muscles on her slender haunches did not relax. Her intense brown eyes followed Amelia across the room.

"Looking forward to Florida, babe?" Dominick asked his wife, his hands sliding down her hips.

"Mmm." She closed her eyes, started grinding her butt against his crotch. "I can't wait to get back to Clearwater Beach, dip my toes in the ocean. It's been too long..."

"I can't wait to dip into *you*."

Cassie made a retching noise. Now it was Folline's turn to elbow *her* in the ribs. Cassie responded with a look that said: *I know, but are you hearing this?*

Heart racing, Amelia staggered to the window as if pulled on an invisible leash.

Petra turned to face her husband. "I know why *you're* itching to hit the road, mister. You can't wait to get your hands on...what's her name again?"

"Giselle."

"That sounds incredibly slutty."

"Fingers crossed."

"She's the redhead, right?"

"Yep."

"He *really* likes redheads," Petra said, looking over at Folline.

Folline sneered at them. Cassie squeezed her hand. They watched Amelia approach the window.

"Did I tell you about her tattoo?" Dominick said. "It's Tinkerbell, pushing a little lawnmower, right above her—"

She nipped at his ear. "God, I get so jealous I want to tear a bitch's eyes out!"

"You'll have your fun with her. Eventually. Once I've had my fill."

"I certainly will."

Amelia heard none of their conversation. She took a deep breath, threw aside the curtain, saw only her petrified reflection staring back at her. She cupped her hands around her eyes, peering through the window.

"Meel," said her friends. "What's out there?"

"Go ahead," Petra said. "Open it." She made a show of fanning herself. "This place could use some fresh air, anyway. I am *parched*."

Amelia struggled with the latch, her hands trembling like skittish creatures with minds of their own.

Finally, she raised the window. A cool breeze wafted into the room, bringing with it a whiff of pine trees and...something else. It made her think of a camping trip with her parents the summer before she started middle school. The smoky smell that tickled her nostrils now reminded her of their firepit the following morning, of ashes and embers and the melancholy sense of an innocent era consumed by flames, leaving nothing to look forward to.

She was also sure she smelled...*gasoline?*

Amelia pressed her face against a thin bug screen with a rip in one corner. The chirping of crickets was almost deafening. Several seconds passed before her eyes adjusted to the darkness outside.

When she saw it, she stumbled back from the window. She clapped a hand over her mouth.

It sat on a patch of scorched earth next to a massive oak stump and an old clothesline stretched between two rusty poles. The charred and blackened husk of a car. The glass in every window had shattered from the heat; it lay sparkling on the ground around the destroyed vehicle.

She recognized it instantly. Her father's Scion. If she had any doubt, the peeling square of an old bumper sticker that had barely survived the flames proved to Amelia what she so desperately wished to deny: a logo for his favorite band on a Union Jack background.

"No," she cried.

A dark shape sat slumped in the driver's seat. It was a hideous, hairless thing. One skeletal hand rested on the steering wheel...

She covered her face with her hands. Started sobbing uncontrollably.

Her friends stood, intending to console her. But the Doberman took a step toward them and barked again. They sat back down. Folline pulled her knees up to her chest, as if the dog couldn't get her as long as her feet didn't dangle off the bed.

"Daddy!" Amelia bawled. "Oh, God...D-Daddy...*why?*"

"Take a seat and we can talk about it," Petra said.

"Fucking psychos!"

"Careful," Dominick said. "You might hurt our feelings."

"What is it, Meel?" Cassie asked.

Amelia stumbled over to them. "He was right there...all along...and we didn't even know."

"Meel?" Folline said. "Tell us. Is it—"

Amelia tasted bitter bile rising in the back of her throat. "They *burned* him."

"Well, *most* of him," Petra said.

"It's impossible to get rid of *everything* unless you own a crematorium," Dominick said.

If not for their lifelong friendship with Folline, neither Amelia nor Cassie would have known what he was talking about right away. Thanks to Folline, they could have taken one glimpse at a dead man and recognized a clear case of carbon-monoxide poisoning (a cherry-red hue to the skin). They could have told you that your hair and fingernails don't *really* continue to grow after you croak (it's just a myth). They also knew the average woodfire burns at nine hundred degrees Fahrenheit, while nearly *two thousand* degrees is required to reduce a cadaver to ash (even then, there are some bones left over that must be pulverized).

"Ugh...my hair still smells like smoke," Petra complained. "Mark my words. Next time we're looking for a lake."

"What a nightmare," said Dominick. "Sure wasn't how I planned to spend my morning."

"You're telling me. I should be in Chicago right now!"

"*What did he ever do to you?*" Amelia screamed at them.

Dominick blinked at her. "That's easy. He was boning my wife!"

That earned another throaty laugh from his better half.

"He got what he deserved."

A dreamy look crossed Petra's face. "It sure was fun while it lasted, though. The things that man could do with his tongue..."

"Don't push it," Dominick said.

Amelia fell into her friends' arms, trembling. "Why? Oh, G-God. D-Daddy...why?"

"That's easy," Dominick said.

"Because adultery is wrong," Petra said with another giggle.

Amelia shot to her feet. "Apparently somebody forgot to give *you* the fucking memo!"

Delilah barked five times fast, as if to say: *Sit your ass back down!*

Amelia's fury overpowered her fear for the next few seconds. She glared at Petra. The dog barked again, took a step toward her.

Cassie pulled Amelia back down on the bed and said, "That's your 'thing,' though, isn't it? You perverts get off on it."

"You...collect people," said Folline. "You make your own death portraits now."

Dominic squeezed his wife's shoulder: *I've got this, babe.*

Petra stepped back, giving him the floor: *By all means, babe.*

Dominick paced from one side of the room to the other as he spoke, like a teacher lecturing a roomful of students. "People today, they just don't get it. But Petra and I figured out the secret to a successful marriage a long time ago. It's simple, really. You gotta keep it *fun*. You can't ever let things get boring. A relationship can survive financial problems. And we can all name at least one pet peeve about our spouse that gets under our skin. For example, you-know-who snores like a goddamn grizzly bear—"

"He's full of it. I don't snore."

"—and, if she'll let me finish, I'm not perfect either. Sometimes, I'll admit, I have a tendency to mansplain. Drives her crazy. My point is...you gotta maintain that *spark*. You gotta find ways to keep the excitement in your marriage. No matter what."

"Have you assholes ever tried ziplining?" Cassie said. "How about scuba diving? It's better than *killing people!*"

"Different strokes," said Dominick.

"Scuba diving?" said Petra. "That's not a bad idea, Dom. We could swim with the sharks!"

"You want me to take you scuba diving, baby? I'll take you anytime you wanna go."

"Promise?"

"Sure."

"Fuck, I love you." Petra grabbed her husband by his shirt, pulled him to her violently.

They kissed. It was a deep, wet one that seemed to last forever. She reached down, stroked his groin with one hand through his jogging shorts.

The teenagers watched them, their faces drained of all color. They gawked at each other in disbelief, as if to say: *We're living in bizarro world. These two, they aren't even human. They're something else, wearing people skin. They are the sharks. And our fear is the blood in the water. They're enjoying every second of this.*

Amelia leaned into Cassie. Her shoulders hitched with sobs, shaking the entire bed. "I can't believe...I said he was *dead* to me."

Cassie stroked the top of her head. "You didn't mean it."

"I didn't understand how he could do that to Mom. But I never wanted anything to happen to him."

"We know, hon. You don't have to tell us."

"Wherever he is now, he knows it too," said Folline.

The couple's tongues untangled.

"Are you hearing this, dear?" Petra said. "Her daddy's in a better place now, he's looking down from Heaven, and he's so *proud* of her!" She shivered, as if touched by the notion. "Wrong. Your daddy doesn't know anything, kid, because he's fucking *dead*."

"Loverboy looked like a piece of beef jerky after we were done with him," said Dominick.

"Screw you!" said Amelia, tears streaming down her face.

"That's not nice." Dominick said. "How can we be friends if you keep talking to us like that?"

"I guess we missed the part where we became friends with you scumbags," Cassie said.

Dominick studied Cassie for a moment. He glanced down at her rainbow bracelet. "I think I've got you figured out. You're some kind of man-hating dyke, aren't you?"

"That might make sense if you were a man. But you're not. You're a piece of shit!"

"My woman will tell you otherwise."

"That's 'cause she's a piece of shit too."

"Watch it," Petra said.

Cassie stood. The Doberman growled at her, but she paid the animal no attention as she shouted, "Who knows what Amelia's dad saw in your nasty ass. Your coochie probably smells like rotten tuna. I'll bet you've got more crabs than Red Lobster. Your left leg called, ho-bag, it said to tell you it misses your right one—"

Petra slapped her across the face. Hard. The sound was like a gunshot in the still, quiet room. Her diamond wedding ring drew blood as it sliced across Cassie's cheek.

Delilah barked again: *Yeah, that's what you get!*

Cassie fell back onto the bed, holding a hand to her wounded cheek.

"You wanna watch your mouth, cunt," Petra said. "Delilah gets tired of Kibbles 'n Bits every day. She'd love to get a taste of you, and I'm the only thing stopping her from eating you alive."

The dog's ears perked up when she heard her name.

Cassie's friends leaned over her. Folline brushed her hair out of her face while Amelia tenderly touched her cheek and said how sorry she was for dragging them into this.

"You should be sorry," Petra said. "Amelia, is it? Just so we're clear, I do know where you live. Maybe we'll pay your mommy a visit when we're done here. We'll spend some time with her before we hit the road and just before I slit her throat, I'll let her know it's all her daughter's fault. Her and her smart-mouth friends who couldn't mind their own fucking business."

"My God, you are a wildcat," Dominick said, pulling his wife back into his arms.

They locked lips again, started slow-dancing to a song only they could hear.

When they were done tonguing each other's tonsils, Petra said, "I'm horny."

"You're always horny," said Dominick.

"Too bad my hubby smells like a high school locker room."

"I could say the same about you."

"Meet me in the shower in five?"

"You know I'm game. But what about our troublemakers?"

"I haven't decided yet what we're gonna do with them," Petra said. "For now...Delilah can handle them just fine, don't you think?"

Judging from his expression, her husband wasn't so sure.

"Delilah will tear them to pieces if they even fucking sneeze. Tell me I'm wrong." She batted her eyelashes at him. "Unless you don't want me."

"You three, get over here," Dominick said. "Against the wall."

Petra laughed, set her vaping mod down on the dresser beside the Polaroid camera.

Amelia and her friends did as they were told, giving the dog a wide berth. Delilah made a wet snuffling noise as they passed her. She laid her head down on her front paws, watching the trio's every move.

"Sit." Dominick said it to the girls this time, pointing at the floor. He closed the bedroom door with a *click*, blocking an easy exit, before heading into the bathroom.

The girls sat on the floor, facing the bed.

"*Pass auf.*" He treated the dog to a quick scratch on top of her head. "Don't let them go anywhere."

The Doberman barked: *I'm on it!*

Petra jogged into the bathroom. "Don't be long, stud-muffin. I'm already soaking wet."

"Oh, damn." Dominick tore off his shirt. "Excuse me, teenyboppers. BRB!"

"I can't believe I said he was yummy," Folline said under her breath.

"What are we gonna do?" Amelia wept.

They watched the couple in the adjacent room. The bathroom door hung ajar. Petra turned on the water, got the temperature just right, then glanced back at the teenagers and blew them a kiss. Without a hint of shame, she peeled off her tight leggings, discarding them like a second skin. She stepped out of her panties, tossed them aside, then pulled off her "SEE NO EVIL" shirt and gray sports bra beneath. Meanwhile, Dominick undressed behind the bathroom door, but if the girls suspected he did so out of modesty, they quickly realized they were mistaken. His pale buttocks appeared in the gap between the door and the threshold. He smacked Petra's ass, and the sound of it echoed off the walls and tile floor. She took his hand and led him into the shower.

Outside, from somewhere in the distance, came the lonely sound of a train's horn wailing through the night.

A minute later the couple were making love right in front of them. Dominick's bright blue eyes stared out at the girls through clouds of steam. Petra arched her back and moaned, her small breasts pressed flat against the shower door as he took her from behind. Flesh squeaked on glass.

"Jesus," Cassie said.

"You guys," Folline whispered. "This is beyond messed up."

"Ya think?"

"They want us to see them," Amelia said.

"Don't give them what they want," Cassie said. "Look at me."

In the bathroom, Petra let out a little squeal.

"What are we gonna do?" Folline said.

"We gotta get out of here," Cassie said.

"But how?"

"One of us has to make a run for it."

"No way." Amelia stared at the dog. The dog stared back from less than six feet away. "That thing will tear us apart."

"So we sit here, wait 'til they get their rocks off, then let them do whatever they plan to do to us?" A thin trickle of blood had seeped from the scratch on Cassie's cheek. She wiped at it with the back of one hand, glanced down at her hand and rubbed it on her sweatpants. "Not this homegirl. I'm not gonna end up in their fucking book."

"We should draw straws."

"Do you *have* any straws, Folline Raine?"

"No. What about rock, paper, scissors?"

"Don't be dumb," said Cassie. "We all know it's gotta be me."

"Cassie," Amelia said. "You'd never get the door open in time—
"

"I'm not going out the door. I'm going through that window."

"You're crazy!" Folline said.

"That screen's in bad shape. If I take a running jump, I can tear right through it. Piece of cake."

"I don't know," Amelia said.

"I'm the only one who stands a chance of making it to the car."

It was a hell of a risk, but they knew she was right. The previous year Cassie had earned a spot on the junior varsity track team, a privilege rarely granted to eighth-graders. She had represented their school in the regional championships, missing out on a third-place trophy in the 400-meter relay by a measly quarter of a second. But could she outrace something with a top speed of over thirty miles per hour, an opponent that was trained to tear out her throat on command?

"If I can get to the car, my phone's in the backseat. I'll have the fuzz swarming this place before these freaks can say *boo-ya*."

Her friends knew she had never dropped her phone in the tub. It had gone to voicemail when Dominic dialed her number because she had turned it off to save the battery before they left Amelia's house. Cassie's phone was *always* dead or close to dying. The other two constantly teased her about it, asking if she had ever heard of a charger cord, but her ability to make the most out of a perpetual 2% rivalled Christ's miracle with fish and loaves before the hungry masses.

"Trust me. I can do this. It's not a perfect plan. But it's all we've got."

"The key's still in it too!" Amelia remembered. "I left it in the ignition."

"That cinches it. I have to try. Maybe I'll ram right through the house. Can you imagine the looks on their stupid faces?"

A burble of nervous laughter passed between them.

Delilah growled, as if sensing a scheme was afoot.

"Hey," Dominick stopped licking Petra's shoulder to call out from the bathroom, "what are you girls whispering about in there?"

"None of your beeswax, dick," Cassie hissed.

"Secret secrets are no fun," Petra said. "Secret secrets hurt someone!"

"We'll see," said Cassie.

"Stuff it, skank," said Folline.

The couple resumed their lovemaking. Petra closed her eyes and told him to slam it in hard. Dominick gave her what she wanted, gripping her by the bun on the back of her head. The shower door rattled.

Cassie held up a fist. "Best friends 'til the end?"

"Ride or die," Amelia and Folline said at the same time.

They bumped knuckles.

Cassie slowly rose to her feet...

The Doberman's lip curled upward, revealing mean yellow teeth.

Cassie took a deep breath, let it out.

In the bathroom, the sounds of coitus grew louder, the rhythm of the couple's lust accelerating as they neared climax.

Cassie pushed off from the wall and sprinted across the room.

The dog snapped at her, missed taking a chunk out of her ankle by less than an inch.

Cassie jumped onto the bed, bounced off the other side, and dove through the window like a swimmer plunging into a bottomless pool. The screen popped out of its frame, offering little resistance, and the teenager flew into the darkness like one of her favorite superheroes.

Her friends heard her hit the ground outside: "Oof!"

Delilah followed, barking furiously. The Doberman scurried onto the bed and leapt through the window, her slender black body becoming one with the night.

Folline and Amelia ran to the window. "Run, Cassie! *Go!*"

"Oh, fuck," Petra said from the bathroom.

"Godammit!" Dominick shouted. "You *had* to have an audience, didn't you?"

"I didn't hear you complaining," Petra said.

"Should we go?" Folline asked Amelia, her hands already gripping the windowsill to pull herself through. "Should we go too? *What do we do?*"

"Do it," Amelia said, her hands cupping Folline beneath her armpits to lift her through the window. "Go! Go *now!*"

Dominick rushed into the bedroom, a towel wrapped around his waist. Petra followed at his heels, pulling on her panties. Dominick shoved Amelia aside, grabbed Folline around the waist before she could get out the window.

"Not so fast, cutie-pie." He got Folline in a chokehold. "I'll snap your neck like a twig. But I won't kill you. I'll leave you paralyzed for the rest of your fucking life."

Petra subdued Amelia the same way. Her naked skin was wet against Amelia's pajama top. "Where do you think you're going, daddy's girl?"

They all watched as Cassie tore through the darkness. *Why was she running toward the woods?* She had obviously panicked once the dog was on her trail, because she was heading in the wrong direction across the wide backyard. The Doberman was already less than six feet behind her. The dog's vicious barks echoed through the night, as if there were more than one out there, a pack of ravenous beasts tracking their terrified prey. Cassie whirled to face the animal. Delilah snarled at Cassie, cornering her against the vehicle.

"Get away from me!" Cassie feinted from left to right, trying to find a path of escape.

"*Bringen,* Delilah!" Dominick yelled.

Cassie darted back toward the house, babbling as she ran: "No, no, no, no, no..."

"Cassie, look out!" her friends cried.

The dog lunged, got hold of her sweatpants. Amelia and Folline could hear the fabric rip, even from this distance.

Cassie changed direction, sprinted back toward the car.

The dog yanked at her leg, growling.

Cassie went down.

"Oops." Petra blew hot breath in Amelia's ear. "It doesn't look good for her now."

"Get off!" Cassie shrieked. "Get off me!"

"Watch what happens next," said Petra.

The Doberman's head whipped from side to side.

Cassie kicked and fought. Somehow she was able to roll over, onto her back. She punched the dog in the side of her head. Delilah yelped, then leapt onto Cassie's chest and sank her teeth into her collarbone.

Cassie screamed.

"Please," Amelia begged the couple. "Call her off. Make her stop!"

"We'll do anything you ask!" Folline cried.

"*Aus,* Delilah," Dominick called through the window. "Drop it."

The dog released Cassie. Cassie cowered beneath her, dark blood pouring from her arm and soaking her Batman tank-top. Tears glistened on her face as she crab-walked away from the beast, pleading for mercy. But then she bumped against the oak stump not far from Brian Fletcher's blackened Scion and she suddenly had nowhere else to go. Delilah took a step toward her, barked in her face, assuring her that this was far from over.

"Please," Cassie cried. "N-No. Get away…"

"You called her off," Petra said to her husband. "Now, why did you do that?"

"After all those nasty things she said to you, I thought you should have the honors."

"How did you ever get to be so sweet?"

"Happy wife, happy life."

"No," Amelia said. "Please don't…"

"Please," Folline sobbed. "We'll tell her to come back inside."

"Wait," Petra said. "One second." She released Amelia. "Dom, don't let her go anywhere."

Dominick grabbed Amelia by the wrist with his free hand.

Petra stepped over to the tripod in the corner, detached the video camera. She slid out the little viewing screen on its side. Pushed a button. A red light on the front blinked to life like a bloodshot eye.

"We'd hate ourselves if we didn't get this."

"Hell, yeah," her husband agreed.

"Don't do this," Folline pleaded.

"She didn't mean it," Amelia said. "She'll come back inside."

"Oh, it's too late for that." Petra gripped Amelia by the back of the neck with one hand, and with the other she held the video camera out the window. "Do it, Delilah. *Packen!*"

The teenagers wailed in terror as the dog lunged at Cassie and tore out her throat.

Her limbs flailed.

Her screams faded to sick wet gurgling sounds.

Then...nothing.

Silence. Even the crickets had stopped chirping for now. As if they too were appalled at what they had witnessed.

"Holy fuck," Dominic said when it was over. "I've never seen anything like that."

"And we've seen some fucked up shit, haven't we, dear?" said Petra.

Dominick released Folline, tweaked one of his wife's stiff nipples before strolling away from the window.

"Bad boy." She released Amelia long enough to fiddle with a button on the camera, zooming in on the carnage as she watched it on the viewing screen with a sadistic gleam in her eye.

"Did you get it all?" Dominick asked her.

"I did. This is *good stuff*, baby..."

Outside, Delilah dragged Cassie's corpse limply across the lawn, like a fallen scarecrow that was missing most of its straw. The dog's muzzle nudged the dead teenager's neck, lapping up the blood that covered her dirty torso.

Petra filmed for another minute or so before turning off the camera. She set it down on the nearby nightstand, between the tube of lubricant and the cock ring. "Can't wait to watch *that* again later. Maybe with some crackers, goat cheese, and a nice glass of pinot noir?"

"You're adorable when you act like a diva," said Dominick.

A shrill ringing filled Amelia's skull. She gnashed her teeth, covered her ears. Tilted her head back and screamed louder than she had ever screamed before.

Folline wrapped her arms around Amelia and joined in.

Petra closed the window, latched it. "Can't let *that* happen again. Jesus Christ, Dom, these bitches are giving me a headache. Did you already pack the Tylenol?"

Amelia pulled Folline away from the window. "Don't look. Don't look at her anymore."

"She got herself pinched, didn't she, Meel? She went and…g-got herself *pinched*."

At first, Amelia didn't get it. For several seconds she was sure Folline had lost her mind, as if witnessing their friend's brutal murder had shattered her sanity and left her a gibbering wreck. But then she was struck with a memory that nearly brought her to her knees beneath a tsunami of soul-crushing grief…

When they were kids, Cassie had been terrified of a next-door neighbor's Doberman. The dog never threatened her—old Shamus was too ancient to do much more than pace back and forth in his pen—but he was the star of numerous bed-wetting nightmares for nine-year-old Cassie. She had been convinced that if a Doberman Pinscher got hold of you, it would slowly *pinch* you to death. Cassie's father explained that the dog's name was merely a nod to some German guy, the first person to ever breed them, and one night he attempted to prove it to her, looking over her shoulder as she pulled it up on Wikipedia. Turned out Mr. McKinley was *half* right. There were several theories on the etymology of the word "pinscher," but most likely it was derived from the French word *pincer*…meaning "to seize, to bite, or to grip." For the next week Cassie refused to sleep anywhere but in her parents' bed. She was sure the bony black demon would leap through her bedroom window in the middle of the night and nip her to death, starting at her toes.

Amelia knew Cassie had remembered old Shamus. How could she not? And yet her desire to save her friends had trumped her childhood fear. That was Cassie for you, selfless to a fault. She was the best person Amelia had ever known. Nobody else came close.

And now she was gone. They would never again paint each other's toenails or braid each other's hair. No more wasting away lazy summer days together swimming at the Y, or Saturday afternoons shopping at Hot Topic for a sick new ensemble. Folline would be forced to find someone else to christen the world's biggest nerd. Amelia would never again talk on the phone for hours on end with her BFF, assuring her that it was *okay* if she didn't like boys and even if her parents were struggling to accept it, there were still two people who loved her more than anything else in the universe.

"Goddamn you!" Amelia screeched at Dominick and Petra. "I hope you rot in Hell!"

"Get back on the bed," Dominick said, unimpressed with her outburst. He was busy pulling clothes off hangers, preparing to get dressed.

The girls obeyed, but as they stumbled across the room Folline taunted him: "Scientists have studied losers like you, you know. They dissected John Wayne Gacy's brain. Bundy's too. Trying to find out what made them tick. But guess what? They didn't find anything wrong. Perfectly normal gray matter. Wanna know why?"

Petra picked up her vaping mod again, took another toke and exhaled cotton candy-scented smoke through her nostrils. "Please. Enlighten us."

"People like you, you're sick in the soul," said Folline. "There's no explanation for it. You're just fucking monsters."

"Is that so?" Dominick dropped his towel, pulled on a pair of boxer briefs.

"You know it's true. You're *proud* of it."

Dominick stepped into a pair of khaki shorts. Petra stuck her arms through the straps of a leopard-spotted bra, then turned around so he could clasp it for her. He kissed the nape of her neck when that was done, pulled a pair of blue jeans from a hanger and handed them to her.

Outside, Delilah started barking again, as if to remind her masters not to forget about her.

Amelia wiped her eyes, shifted position on the bed, trying to figure out a way to buy some time. She cleared her throat. When she spoke, her voice was hoarse, her throat raw from screaming.

"Can I ask you a question?"

Petra raised an eyebrow as she pulled on her jeans.

"Did he ever talk about…leaving her?"

Petra didn't answer at first. She looked around the room, searching for something.

"I need to know. Did he ever say anything about wanting to divorce my mom so he could be with you?"

"Meel," Folline said, "Does it make any difference? That wasn't her goal, anyway."

Amelia ignored her.

Petra sighed. "Fine. If it makes you feel any better, your father had a change of heart."

"What?"

"He decided he wanted to break it off with me."

Amelia's mouth hung open.

"Close your mouth, sweetie, you look like a fish," Petra said. "He dropped by to tell me this morning, on his way to the airport. Said he couldn't do this anymore to 'the missus.' He'd been feeling guilty for a while, planned to come clean about everything as soon as he got back from his trip."

Amelia was speechless. She thought about her awkward conversation with Dad the night before, when she called Tyler Thompson a cheating d-bag. Did that have anything to do with his "change of heart?" Perhaps her not-so-subtle censure came through loud and clear?

Petra walked to the dresser, started pulling out the drawers one by one. When she saw each one was empty, she slammed it closed again, obviously growing more and more frustrated as she failed to find what she was looking for. "'Poor little wifey, she doesn't deserve this,' he said. 'She's a good woman, I made a mistake, and I wish I could take it all back,' he said. 'If some douchebag did this to my daughter, I would want to kick his ass.' Blah, blah, blah…"

A tear trickled down Amelia's cheek. She wiped it away with her pajama sleeve.

"Funny…I don't remember him worrying too much about the wifey when I was sitting on his face."

Once again, Amelia tasted bile rising in the back of her throat.

"Here's the thing, though. I don't get dumped. *I'm* the one who does the dumping."

Dominick threw on a purple silk shirt, said, "She doesn't take rejection well."

"Not to mention, I *really* wanted to see Wrigley Field."

"Any more questions?" Dominick asked.

Amelia stared down at the floor, shook her head.

"Darling," Petra said, "have you seen my favorite blouse? The burgundy one? I've looked everywhere for it."

"It was in the closet, right?"

"It was. It's not now. We're not going anywhere until I find that blouse, Dom. It's a Chanel."

"Maybe you packed it?"

Petra's eyes grew wide as she noticed something on the floor, between the bed and the window. "The *fuck?*"

She bent, picked up her blouse. It was wrinkled, had a small rip in the shoulder.

"Oh, shit," said Dominick.

"Did you do this?" Petra asked Amelia. "Oh, you are going to pay." She cradled the piece of clothing as if it were a stillborn child. "Dom. My favorite blouse. They murdered it!"

"Sorry, babe. I'll buy you another one. Maybe we can stop by one of those outlet malls and—"

"You should be more upset about this. I bought this on our honeymoon!"

"I remember," Dominick said.

Petra spotted the jug of bleach then, where Amelia had stashed it at the base of the tripod. She picked it up. The liquid inside made a sloshing sound. She looked down at the jug. Back at Amelia. An understanding dawned in her expression. Her face burned bright pink.

"Oh, you ruthless little *twat*."

Amelia raised her chin defiantly, refusing to break eye contact with her.

"You're not as innocent as you look, are you, daddy's girl? Serious anger issues."

"I just wanted you to leave him alone," Amelia said. "I thought if I could scare you off things could go back to the way they used to be."

"Scared yet, baby?" Dominick asked his wife.

"Shaking from head to toe." Petra yawned, glanced at the Fitbit on her wrist. "What time is it? Fuck! We should have been on the road two hours ago, Dom! Guess who's *not* driving 'cause she needs her beauty sleep?"

"Not a problem. I'll pop one or two of those dexies we got off Janice. I'll be good through tomorrow afternoon."

"Great. Be a dear, would you, and fetch me that baseball bat I saw in the living room? Meanwhile, I'll finish packing."

"On it." Dominick opened the bedroom door, disappeared down the hallway.

Amelia and Folline exchanged a desperate look: *We gotta make a move. NOW.* But what were they supposed to do? No one could hear them no matter how loudly they screamed. The couple's closest neighbors were several miles away; it didn't take a genius to know that was why they had rented this house. They had torched her father's car here, for God's sake, presumably with no more fear of discovery than two people enjoying a backyard fish fry.

"People know we're here," Amelia blurted out. "People know we're here and they're gonna come looking for us, and when they do, you're gonna be in a shit-heap of trouble!"

Petra laughed. "I suppose Mommy and Daddy have no problem with you running around raising hell past your bedtime, destroying other people's property like a bunch of niggers."

"Racists too," Folline said. "You're disgusting."

"Let's see how disgusting you think I am when I yank out your tongue and feed it to my dog so you can't run that mouth anymore. Assuming she's still hungry, after having her way with your girlfriend."

Amelia let out an anguished moan.

Folline gave the woman no more backtalk.

From the backyard came another round of muffled barks, as if Delilah were begging the couple to let her in for dessert.

Petra slid a black valise from the top shelf of the closet, sang "Who Let the Dogs Out" under her breath as she started packing up the cameras, the cock-ring, and the tube of K-Y jelly.

Folline sniffled, said, "Meel...?"

"Yeah?"

"Joey's gonna be so upset, isn't he? Cassie never got to put her Punisher rip-off to bed."

Amelia stared at her. Folline stared back, with eyes that were red and swollen from crying. Once again, Amelia feared her friend had gone off the deep end, and even if they lived through this, she was destined to spend the rest of her days bouncing off the walls of a rubber room in the mental hospital over in Morganton.

But suddenly she understood. She realized Folline was trying to communicate something to her, something only she could comprehend...and she could almost hear an audible *click* in her brain as each piece of the puzzle fell into place.

Joey's gonna be so upset. Cassie never got to put her Punisher rip-off to bed....

"Joey" was Folline's big brother. These days he preferred "Joseph," but Folline's friends called him Joey because they'd known him by that name since he was a kid. And because he hated it.

For the past couple of years, Cassie had been working on her own comic book. Her talent was undeniable, but neither of her pals had the heart to tell her that the story's protagonist was derivative of an already-iconic superhero.

It wasn't the Punisher who had inspired Arachnid Gal…but the message hidden in Folline's words couldn't have been clearer.

Joey's gonna be so upset. Cassie never got to put her Punisher rip-off to bed...

Amelia's heart slammed in her chest. Folline saw in her friend's expression that she understood, and she slowly nodded.

The last Walmart bag. At some point it must have been kicked beneath the bed.

Along with one final, unopened can of spray paint…it held the Punisher knife they had "borrowed" from Joey.

Amelia returned Folline's nod.

"Who's Joey?" Petra asked, stepping inside the bathroom for a moment to shove their sweaty exercise attire into the valise. "What does that mean?"

"Cassie was working on a book," Amelia said. "Her dream project." Thinking fast: "Folline's brother loved it. Now she'll never get to finish it. Thanks to you assholes."

"Hmm," Petra said, folding up the tripod. "That's too bad. Tell him to take it up with Delilah. See how that works out for Joey."

Dominick entered the room again, with Amelia's baseball bat slung over one shoulder.

"Put me in coach, I'm ready to play," he said, miming a slow-motion swing at the teenagers' faces.

"Me first," Petra said. "Daddy's girl needs to learn a lesson about sticking her nose in other people's business."

He offered her the bat.

She paused. "No. I've got a better idea."

She stood over Amelia. Lifted the jug of bleach. In her other hand, she held her ruined blouse. She screwed the cap off the jug. Wadded the end of a sleeve into a little ball and stuck it down inside. Liquid sloshed again as she tipped the jug, soaking the fabric.

"Please," Folline said, "just let us go…"

"Daddy's girl. Open your mouth."

"No," said Amelia.

"Do what I tell you, or I will hold you down and this will be a lot worse. I'll empty this whole fucking jug somewhere else. Starting with those pretty green eyes."

"Leave her alone!" Folline cried.

"I've always wanted to do this," Petra said. "Just to see what will happen. But not too much. Just a little bit at first…"

Folline slid down the edge of the bed, her butt thumping hard onto the floor. "I don't wanna die! Please, just let us go!"

"Not so brave anymore, are you?" Petra said.

Outside, the Doberman barked again, followed by another lonely whine.

"P-Please," Folline said, tears streaming down her face. "I just wanna go home. I never asked for this. I wish I never came here. Amelia, you talked us into this and Cassie's dead and now they're gonna kill us too."

"Folline, I'm sorry," Amelia said.

"This is all your fault," Folline sobbed. "I *hate* you."

It was an Oscar-worthy performance, Amelia thought. She knew Folline could fib like a pro when she needed to, but this was a far cry from the single line she had spoken in an eighth-grade production of *Our Town*. This was different from that time when they'd played with a Ouija board and she pretended to be possessed by an evil spirit. Lying to her parents about a sleepover at Cassie's house last New Year's Eve so she could hang out with Nathan Kendall, that was one thing. This was life-or-death. Was her caterwauling enough to fool their captors? Would it distract them long enough for Folline to feel around behind her back and find the knife before they knew what she was up to? *Where did we drop the bag? What if she's not even close?* The couple was sure to catch on any second...

"You listening to this?" Petra said. "You screwed the pooch when you decided to fuck with me, daddy's girl. You're gonna die knowing you lost *two* friends in one night. I almost feel sorry for you."

"Please," Folline sobbed. "I just want my parents to come get me. I'm too young to die!"

"Dom, honey...wanna tell Red what her chances are, trying to appeal to my better nature?"

"Not good," Dominick said.

"The first person I ever killed was my sister, after my man here popped her cherry. It was an accident, I didn't mean to hold that pillow over her face as long as I did, but that's what you get when you mess with my fella. I haven't shed a tear for Vicky in fifteen years. You think I give two shits about you little bitches?" She leaned over Amelia and sprayed her face with spittle as she bellowed: "I'm not gonna tell you again to open your fucking mouth!"

Folline sniveled and whimpered, snot bubbling from her nostrils and dripping down her chin as she tried to reach the knife under the bed. "Please...you don't have to do this!"

Amelia winced when she heard the Walmart bag rustle. She was quite sure she heard the knife clank against the paint can too.

Folline let out a long, quavering howl.

"Dominick, will you *please* shut her up? I've got my hands full here."

Petra grabbed Amelia by the hair, forcing her head back. The bleach-soaked blouse lay wet against Amelia's cheek as the lunatic gripped her chin with her other hand. Her thumb wormed its way between Amelia's lips, tasting of bleach and bodywash. Amelia gagged. Fumes burned her eyes.

Dominick approached Folline with the Louisville Slugger. "You ready for this, doll? I'm gonna turn that pretty face into something not so fine."

He reared back with the bat, like A-Rod preparing to hit a homerun.

"How many hits do you think it will take?" he asked his wife.

"I don't know," said Petra. "Just do it. Put a fucking dent in her skull."

In an instant, Folline's crying ceased. She sucked up snot mid-sob, as if she were a faucet suddenly deprived of its water supply...

...and she brought the knife out from under the bed, stabbing it into Dominick's crotch in one savage thrust.

He dropped the bat. Fell to his knees. For several seconds he gawped at her, his mouth working soundlessly. And then he looked down at his ruined genitals, and he began to scream. It was a high-pitched, almost feminine shriek. The knife was plunged into his groin all the way to the hilt.

"Baby?" Petra released Amelia, knocked over the jug of bleach as she rushed to her husband's side. It gurgled onto the carpet, filling the room with its pungent chlorine stench. She knelt beside Dominick, running her hands over his lap as if she could somehow piece his private parts back together with the power of love.

"Oh, Dom...oh, no...do you want me to take it out, baby? Should I...*what should I do?*"

All of the color had drained from Dominick's face. He rolled onto his side, and his screams faded to incoherent babbling as he pulled the knife out. Blood spurted from his genitals, soaking through his khaki shorts and streaming down his calves. He stared down at the blade as if it were an old friend who had done him wrong. It slid from his palm and thumped onto the carpet.

"What'd they do to me?" he rasped, in a voice that sounded as if it belonged to a man three times his age.

Delilah's barks grew louder than ever on the other side of the window, a frenetic machine-gun barrage that went on and on as if the beast were some supernatural hellhound that had no need to catch its breath. The Doberman's claws scratched frantically at the vinyl siding as she tried to climb the wall to get inside.

"I'm sorry they hurt you, baby," Petra cried, holding her husband's head in her hands. "Tell me how I can make it better..."

"K-Kill them," Dominick wheezed. "Slow..."

Petra started to rise, but Amelia jumped off the bed, onto her back. She grabbed the woman by the hair, slammed her face into the floor. But once the teenager had lost the element of surprise, Petra threw her off with a roar.

Amelia flew across the room. The back of her head slammed into the side of the dresser.

Petra stood, lurched over to Amelia like a monster in a horror flick. Her wet blonde hair hung in her face. Her teeth were bared. Her hands, now covered with her husband's blood, curled into talons as she reached for Amelia.

"Fucking bitch!" Her hands wrapped around Amelia's throat.

Amelia thrashed beneath her.

"Hurt *my* husband? You're gonna fucking *die*..."

From behind Petra, a metallic rattling sound: *Chocka-chocka-chocka*.

"Hey, psycho," Folline said. "Look what I got."

Petra turned...

...and Folline blasted her pointblank in the face with the red spray paint. The can hissed. The paint coated Petra's teeth and tongue, dripped down her cheeks and chin, spackled her chest and shoulders before she could throw up an arm to block the assault. She crashed into a nightstand with a maniacal screech, knocking over a lamp.

"Meel, are you okay?"

"I think so." Amelia coughed as Folline helped her to her feet.

Petra flailed about, temporarily blinded. She rubbed frantically at her eyes. Her face was a satanic Halloween mask. "Fuck with me! You're gonna regret that! Make you cunts wish you were never fucking born!"

Her sticky hands got hold of Amelia's pajama top.

Folline picked up the baseball bat, swung it into the side of Petra's skull. Petra went limp, bounced off the bed face-first, marking the mattress like a human stamp with a crimson print of her scowling features. She hit the floor and lay still, on her side, as if she were peering under the bed in hopes of finding another Walmart bag full of makeshift weapons.

Amelia scrambled across the room, going for the knife.

Dominick grabbed it first. He mumbled something that sounded like: "Were just having fun..."

"Gimme, prick. That belongs to my brother."

She snatched the knife from him, slicing his palm open to the bone as she did so. He yelped. She handed the knife to Amelia.

"No! You leave him alone!"

Petra was back on her feet. She ran at them again.

Folline bunted her in the face with the bat. Something crunched. Her nose flattened. She wobbled drunkenly but remained standing. Folline hit her again.

Petra collapsed. Twitched once...then lay sprawled on the carpet in a prone position without another sound.

"That was for Cassie, bitch!"

Amelia stared down at her archenemy, her hands shaking. "Is she—"

"Sorry," Folline said. "She should have been yours."

"It doesn't matter," Amelia said. "It's not about that anymore."

Delilah had finally stopped barking outside. Now the night was filled with a mournful baying, as if the dog knew what was happening and she could do nothing to stop it.

Dominick grabbed Amelia's leg.

She stumbled, pulled away from him. The blood-drenched carpet made a sick squelching sound beneath her shoes.

His flesh was gray. He pointed a quivering finger at her. "Kill you both," he wheezed. "Just...gimme a minute..."

With some effort, he got to his knees.

He lunged for Amelia.

She stuck the knife in his chest, aiming for his heart.

He fell back. His head struck the wall, knocking a hole in the sheetrock.

Amelia stood over him, her chest heaving in and out. She flinched when Folline touched her shoulder.

Dominick's hand came up, as if he might try to pull the knife out of his heart. It hovered in the air for a moment, his fingers twitching, but then flopped to the floor. His eyes rolled up into the back of his head.

"Pretty sure he's toast," Folline said. "There ain't no coming back from that."

"Yeah," Amelia said. "Her too?"

"Looks that way. What do we do now, Meel?"

"We go home."

Folline took one of Amelia's blood-sticky hands in her own. "Best idea I've heard all night."

Excerpt from transcript of 911 call (August 8, 2020 @ 12:24 a.m.):

Dispatcher: The people who did this, you're sure they're deceased?
Caller: Yeah…(unintelligible)
Dispatcher: Should you wait outside until help arrives, just in case?
Caller: We can't do that. There's a dog outside.
Dispatcher: A dog, you said?
Caller: It killed our friend. Her name was Cassie. She never hurt anyone, and they sicced their dog on her.
Dispatcher: I'm sorry. Sit tight for me, okay? Officers are en route.
Caller: Yeah. Okay. Please hurry.
(sound of a dog barking in the background)

The night was alive with the swirling lights of emergency vehicles. The air smelled of blood and diesel fumes. Yellow police tape marked the perimeter of the crime scene, its stark yellow contrasting with the ribbons of toilet paper drooping from the house and trees like decorations for some ill-fated party. Tall portable lamps had been erected in each corner of the property, their bright white glow pushing back the shadows like bullies forcing smaller things to scatter. Uniformed police officers snapped photos of the vandalism while others carried items out of the house in clear plastic EVIDENCE bags. A woman wearing latex gloves removed the luggage from the Pathfinder's cargo hold.

An ambulance was parked in the road, its engine rumbling quietly. Its rear doors hung open. Folline and Amelia sat on the curb about thirty feet away, being examined by two paramedics. One of them, a chubby guy in his early twenties who smelled like he had taken a bath in cheap cologne, had asked Folline if the pentagram on her shirt meant she was "some kinda devil worshipper." Without missing a beat, she replied, "Absolutely." His partner, a pretty Hispanic lady, shined a penlight in Amelia's eyes, confirming that she didn't have a concussion via a series of questions like *What's today's date* and *Do you know where you are?* ("47 Callaghan Drive," Amelia responded to the latter almost defiantly; even after she grew old and senile, she would never forget this place).

"Some kinda night, huh, Meel?" Folline said.

"Some kinda night," Amelia agreed.

A man in a dark suit and tie ducked under the police tape, approaching the teens with long-legged strides. He was a tall black man with the biggest hands the girls had ever seen. He had introduced himself earlier as Detective Mills.

"Ladies." The detective squatted down to chat with them face to face. "How are you holding up?"

Neither of the girls said anything, unsure how to respond. The paramedics finished their business and briskly walked away.

"Just wanted to let you know we haven't forgotten about you. Give me ten minutes, we'll get you out of here. We called your parents. They're meeting us at the station."

"Awesome," Folline said dryly.

Amelia glanced over at her father's Roadrunner, which was being admired by two cops who looked barely old enough to be out of high school.

"Okay, then," said Detective Mills. He rose, started to walk away with his giant hands in his pockets, then stopped. "For the record, you two should be proud. Can't say I condone the vandalism, but...these were bad people."

They stared at him, waiting to learn something they didn't already know.

"That makes you heroes."

He left them with that, stalking across the yard to converse with his partner, a man wearing thick glasses and a blond ponytail.

"I don't feel like a hero," Amelia said.

A muscular cop walked from the back of the house, carrying Delilah's slack form in his arms. The dog's skinny black legs bounced against his hip as he eased her body into the back of an ANIMAL CONTROL truck. The Doberman might have been dead or perhaps just tranquilized. Impossible to tell. The officer banged on the side of the vehicle with a fist and it drove away.

"That fucking dog," said Folline.

For the next few minutes, they watched the chaos around them without speaking.

Then Amelia said, "I can't believe she's gone."

"Same."

"I keep expecting her to walk up any second and sit down beside us."

"She'd probably make some dumb joke about how we ought to do this again next weekend, but maybe we could tee-pee Principal Parker's place instead of messing around with a couple of psycho killers."

"Oh God, that sounds like Cassie."

"Right?" Folline said. "She'd point at that cop over there and say he looks like Ben Stiller."

Amelia laid her head on Folline's shoulder. Folline played with her friend's hair, twirling a curl around one finger.

"Meel?"

"Yeah?"

"I didn't mean what I said in there. It was all part of the act. I don't blame you. I love you."

"I know that, dummy," said Amelia.

A black van arrived, its brakes whining like an overworked beast of burden as it parked beneath the streetlight at the edge of the property. OFFICE OF THE MEDICAL EXAMINER read the logo on its side. A stern-faced woman with a platinum-blonde pixie cut climbed out. She spoke briefly with Detective Mills and his partner. Mills said something that made the woman glance over at Folline and Amelia, and her hard expression melted into one of sympathy. She nodded, climbed back into her van, and drove it around to the back of the house.

"How does it feel knowing that's gonna be you one day?" Amelia said.

"What do you mean?" asked Folline.

"Pulling up at a crime scene in the middle of the night. Loading bodies for autopsies. Solving cases left and right while the men stand around with their thumbs up their butts."

Folline made a scoffing sound. "Not sure if I want that anymore, to be honest. After tonight, I don't think I'd have the stomach for it."

"Don't say that. Don't you dare say that. If you decide to back out now, I might just kick your ass."

"Why?"

"Now more than ever, I think you have to. I think you were born to do it. To help put away monsters like...Dominick and Petra."

"Maybe you're right," Folline said.

"I know I'm right," said Amelia.

"One thing's for sure," said Folline. "I could go the rest of my life without ever smelling cotton candy again."

"Word."

They bumped knuckles.

Both girls sat up with a start when the front door of the house banged open.

Two paramedics eased a stretcher down the steps and across the yard. They were accompanied by the muscular cop who had carried the dog away; he kept pace with the EMTs, one hand on the holster of his gun.

On the gurney: A glimpse of blonde hair, matted with blood and sweat and red spray paint. Their patient's head rolled limply to one side. Her eyelids fluttered...

...and she looked right at Folline and Amelia.

"Wait a minute," Folline said. "That skag is still alive?"

Amelia sighed. "Nothing gets past you, Folline Raine."

Because that was exactly what Cassie would say.

"The only thing they loved more than each other…was MURDER!!!"
— blurb on the front cover of *Fatal Affairs:*
The Story of America's Most Notorious Couple
by Sadie Hartmann

From *USA Today* (August 10, 2020):

FBI: "SERIAL KILLER COUPLE" SUSPECTED OF 12 MURDERS, MAYBE MORE
HEROIC TEENS END SPREE AFTER NIGHT OF HORROR

Asheville, NC - Two teenage girls survived and a third was killed Friday night during an encounter with a couple investigators blame for "at least" a dozen murders in Georgia, North Carolina, Maryland, and Washington, DC. The youths' names have been withheld to protect their identities.

Dominick John Andrade, 34, was mortally wounded by the teenagers during their escape. His wife, Petra Somer Andrade, 33, is currently being treated for "serious injuries," according to the Federal Bureau of Investigation. Petra Andrade will be transferred to the Buncombe County Jail to await indictment upon her release from the hospital.

The investigation is ongoing.

From *USA Today* (April 5, 2021):

SERIAL SEDUCTRESS SENTENCED TO DEATH

Asheville, NC - Jurors deliberated for only two hours yesterday before convicting Petra Andrade, 33, on six counts of first-degree murder, seven counts of accessory to first-degree murder, three counts of first-degree kidnapping, and two counts of desecration of human remains. Judge Steve Thompson subsequently sentenced Andrade to execution by lethal injection, stating, "I have never seen such depravity in thirty years behind the bench, (and) I doubt I ever will."

In collusion with her late husband, Andrade instigated affairs throughout multiple states along the eastern seaboard, ultimately murdering each of her lovers after a period of several months. The couple often captured their gruesome crimes on camera, prompting prosecutors to call them "swingers from Hell."

Andrade's lawyers claimed throughout her trial that their client acted under "extreme" duress at the hands of an abusive spouse. They have filed for appeal.

From *The Asheville Citizen-Times* (May 1, 2021):

FRIENDS HONOR FALLEN "SUPERHERO"

Cassie McKinley dreamed of creating comic books for a living. Her sketchbook and set of colored pencils were never far from reach. She was a self-proclaimed "nerd chick" whose home away from home was Galaxies Unknown, her local comic shop.

Time after time, her beloved crimefighters vanquished the villains who attempted to harm the innocent and the good guys lived happily ever after. But the real world doesn't always work that way. On August 7, 2020, Cassandra Anne McKinley was murdered at fifteen years old.

Cassie's friends and family refused to let her dream die with her. They joined forces this summer to raise funds via the online platform Kickstarter, in hopes of printing enough copies of her work to send to every publisher in the business. "Cassie might not be here to see it," said her best friend Amelia Fletcher, "but she's gonna sell a million copies if it's the last thing we do." Folline Raine, who insisted *she* was Cassie's BFF, added, "Todd McFarlane, watch your back."

The girls' campaign was highly successful, yielding more than its goal, but their adventure doesn't end there. Thanks to the power of social media, word of their tribute reached several top-tier industry professionals, including Diamond Comic Distributors. Diamond is the world's largest distributor of comics and graphic novels, serving retailers all over the world. The company holds exclusive rights with nearly every major comic book publisher.

Cassie McKinley's dream will soon come true. By the end of the year, her book will be available in comic shops across the globe. Her parents plan to donate one hundred percent of the profits to the National Center for Victims of Crime, in their daughter's name.

90 ACTION-PACKED PAGES!!!
ART AND STORY BY Cassandra McKinley
#1
RIDE OR DIE
WTF
GIRL POWER!

THE END

THE AUTHOR GIVES SPECIAL THANKS TO THE FOLLOWING BFFs: Glenda Newman, Carissa Praytor, Audrey West, Somer Canon, Kenzie Jennings, Kristin Dearborn, Sarah French, Mark Allan Gunnells, Steve Saldutti, Donn Gash, John P. Collins Jr, Megan Foley, Mark Steensland, Bradley Esqueda, Mike McClure, Debbie Davidson-Callaghan, Alex McVey, and the members of Optic Oppression.

ABOUT THE AUTHOR

James Newman's published works include the novels *Midnight Rain, The Wicked, Animosity,* and *Ugly As Sin,* the collections *People Are Strange* and *The Long N' Short Of It,* and the novella *Odd Man Out.* He has also co-authored several fan-favorite collaborations, including *Dog Days O' Summer* (with Mark Allan Gunnells), *In The Scrape,* and *The Special* (both with Mark Steensland). *The Special* was recently adapted as a major motion picture by direction B. Harrison Smith (*Death House*), and can be viewed on most major streaming platforms. James lives in North Carolina with his wife and their two sons. When he isn't writing, he loves listening to rock n' roll and watching horror flicks or UNC basketball. Sometimes all at once, because life is short.

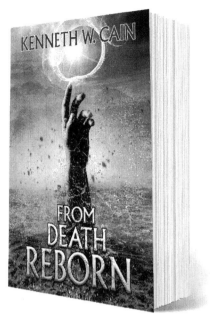

As the clock's pendulum steadily counts down towards the midnight hour, the growing scent of brimstone hangs heavy in the air. The universal symbol of all that is evil, the pentagram, or the inverted pentacle, has been carved in the hardwood floor. Its shape is often described as the goat of lust attacking the Heavens with its horns during the witches' sabbat. Five obsidian candles flicker as the incantations begin. Who will be summoned during this unholy evening? Will it be Baphomet? Or Belial? Maybe even Lucifer himself? The roof timbers groan. Stressed plaster drops to the floor. The demon approaches, holding its ancient grimoire filled with evil stories, written in blood...and here they are.

THE CRUCIFIXION EXPERIMENTS

Jake Mercer's life is spiraling out of control. As a criminal profiler and one of the senior homicide investigators in the Oakland Police Department, he's spent the last twenty-five years getting inside the heads of killers and trying to understand the way they think. He's the best at what he does, but constantly playing in the minds of madmen carries a heavy price, leaving Jake an out of shape, alcoholic loner suspended from active duty.

THE MURDERS HAVE STARTED...

Another serial killer is prowling the streets now, a violent lunatic who's making a game of nailing retired Catholic priests to trees and bridges and hydro poles around the city. Torture and murder isn't enough, the predator experimenting with the bodies of his victims to further whatever diabolical plan only they seem to know.

THE EXPERIMENTS HAVE BEGUN...

Broken down or not, Lieutenant Mercer just might be the only man who can catch this killer before the frightened citizens of Oakland start to panic. Reinstated back onto the force and trying his best to stay out of the bottle, Jake finds himself teamed up with two rookie detectives in what will be his most difficult case ever, and quite possibly his last.

Printed in Great Britain
by Amazon

75079858R00066